Meet **Sparkle**. This five-month-old spaniel mix is just longing for a home. You'll fall in love with her beautiful chestnut-brown-and-white soft fur and long floppy ears. Although she is sweet, she is full of puppy energy and will require a good deal of training. But Sparkle appears ready to learn and is treat motivated. She would be a great addition to any home—the perfect best friend for a little boy or girl to grow up with.

Meet **Hank**. Don't let his gray muzzle fool you. This retriever mix has plenty of joy left in him. He certainly hasn't let the fact that he only has three legs get him down. An owner surrender, Hank is obviously missing the only home and family he's ever known but is still delighted to meet new people. He's been overlooked for a while but we're hoping the right person will see all the love this sweet boy still has left to give.

* * *

FUREVER YOURS: Finding forever homes—and hearts!—has never been so easy.

Dear Reader,

Right now my supersweet two-year-old dog, Flash, who looks like a mini German shepherd, is asleep beside me on the sofa. My cat, a black-and-white beauty named Cleo, is curled up against Flash's back, one white paw on his head. I love these two so much and can barely remember life before I adopted them. Cleo came from our local humane society, and Flash from an all-breed rescue organization that saved him from a crowded county shelter.

Special Edition's new six-book series, Furever Yours, means so much to me. Set around an animal shelter in North Carolina, Furever Yours is all about how we rescue pets and they rescue us right back. My heroine, Claire, volunteers at the Furever Paws Animal Shelter, and when her first love, the man who broke her heart, comes in to adopt a puppy for his little niece, *a lot* of hearts get rescued in the process.

I hope you enjoy Claire and Matt's love story and spending time with the special cast of four-legged (and three-legged) characters in the book! Feel free to visit my website at melissasenate.com for more information on me and my books. And if you follow me on Facebook and @melissasenate on Twitter, you'll see lots of photos of my beloved Flash and Cleo.

Happy New Year,

Melissa Senate

A New Leash on Love

Melissa Senate

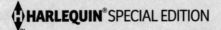

HARLEQUIN® SPECIAL EDITION

Special thanks and acknowledgment are given to
Melissa Senate for her contribution to
the Furever Yours miniseries.

Recycling programs
for this product may
not exist in your area.

ISBN-13: 978-1-335-57360-5

A New Leash on Love

Copyright © 2018 by Harlequin Books S.A.

For questions and comments about the quality of this book,
please contact us at CustomerService@Harlequin.com.

www.Harlequin.com

Printed in U.S.A.

Melissa Senate has written many novels for Harlequin and other publishers, including her debut, *See Jane Date*, which was made into a TV movie. She also wrote seven books for Harlequin's Special Edition line under the pen name Meg Maxwell. Her novels have been published in over twenty-five countries. Melissa lives on the coast of Maine with her teenage son; their rescue shepherd mix, Flash; and a lap cat named Cleo. For more information, please visit her website, melissasenate.com.

Visit the Author Profile page
at Harlequin.com for more titles.

Dedicated with appreciation to animal shelters
and rescue organizations worldwide.

Thank you for all you do.

Chapter One

The gray-muzzled, three-legged Lab mix gnawing on a chew toy in his kennel at the Furever Paws Animal Rescue sure reminded Matt Fielding of himself. The dog was big, and so was Matt, at six foot one, with muscles honed by the United States Army. Matt wasn't missing a leg, but he'd come scarily close, an IED injuring him to the point that he'd been medically retired three months ago, spending that time—until yesterday—in base rehab. He had only a slight limp now, but kneeling down in front of the old dog's kennel had taken a good fifteen seconds.

I'd take you home in a heartbeat, Hank, he thought, his gaze on the dog's chart. The ten-year-old was an "owner surrender." Among the sadder words, for sure. His heart went out to the old guy stuck in this limbo be-

tween homes—like Matt was. But his sister would kill
him if he walked through the door of her pristine house
with a huge senior dog. And getting on her bad side right
now wasn't a good idea.

The former army corporal had his order—and it
was to find his sister's eight-year-old daughter, Matt's
adored niece, Ellie, a suitable puppy. Suitable, of course,
was a relative term. Old Hank might have spoken to
Matt's soul, but he wasn't here to find himself a dog.
Pets required commitment and a solid home, not a guy
who had no idea where he'd be a week or two from now.
Thirty-six and his life up in the air. If anyone had told
Matt, so focused from the time he joined the army at
eighteen, that one day he'd be at a loss for what came
next, he wouldn't have believed it. Until three months
ago, he *was* the US Army. Now, he was a civilian. With
a slight limp.

*It's barely noticeable and is symbolic of your ser-
vice, so don't let it get you down*, his sister had said
yesterday when he'd arrived back in his hometown of
Spring Forest, North Carolina, for the first time in five
years. Little Ellie had saluted him, and he'd swept her
up in a hug. But living in his sister's guest room, despite
his adorable niece telling him knock-knock jokes that
made no sense but still made him laugh, wasn't ideal.
He needed to figure out what came next.

Right now, though, he needed to focus on his mission. *One thing at a time, one moment at a time*, his
doc and the nurses at the rehab had said over and over.

So, back to suitable pups.

"Hank is one of my favorites," a woman said, and
Matt almost jumped.

He knew that voice. He turned to the left and looked up, and standing not ten feet away was Claire Asher.

Claire.

From the look on her beautiful face, it was obvious she hadn't realized it was him. For a moment he couldn't find his voice. All he could do was take in the sight of her, his chest tight and his throat closed. He'd spent so many nights over the past eighteen years thinking about her, wondering how she was, where she was, if she was happy, his memories getting him through some iffy times. And now she stood almost within reach, pale brown eyes wide, mouth dropped open.

She had a leash in her hand and a big cinnamon-colored dog in a purple polka-dotted harness beside her. *A boxer, maybe?* Matt wondered, finding it easier to focus on the dog than the woman—who was staring at him with the same shock that had to be on his face.

"Matt?" she said, wonder in her voice.

The dog next to her tilted her head, his dark-brown ears flopping to the right.

He nodded and stood up, which took the same fifteen seconds getting down had. "I'm here to find a dog for my niece." Going through his mind was, *You look amazing. How are you? I've thought about you constantly. What are you doing here? I've missed you.* Thank God none of that had come rushing out of his mouth.

"Ellie," she said, surprising him. "I've run into your sister a few times over the years."

He nodded, his gaze going to her left hand. No ring. Hadn't he heard she'd gotten married a while back?

"You look great, Claire." She really did. Tall and as slender as she'd been back in high school, she was the

Claire Asher he remembered—would never forget. Her silky, wavy, light blond hair was shoulder-length instead of halfway down her back, and the faintest of crinkles at the corners of those green eyes spoke of the passage of years. The last time he'd seen Claire she was seventeen. Now, she was thirty-five.

"Are you on leave?" she asked.

He shook his head. "I'm a civilian now. Just got back in town yesterday. I'm staying with my sister for a bit. In fact, my sister is why I'm here. She and her husband promised Ellie a puppy for her birthday next month, so I told Laura I'd scout it out. I heard great things about Furever Paws just from asking about pet shelters at the coffee shop."

Claire beamed. "It's a very special place. I volunteer here." She gave the dog beside her a pat. "This is Dempsey. I'm fostering her until she finds a forever home."

"A *furever* home," he said, pointing at the rectangular wooden sign on the wall with the message in silver script: *Where furbabies find their furever homes.*

She smiled—that beautiful Claire Asher smile that used to drive him wild.

"If only you'd come in yesterday or this morning," she said. "Every Saturday and Sunday we hold adoption events here at the shelter. Four puppies found forever—*furever*—homes, plus five adult dogs and five cats."

"So these dogs in the kennels weren't chosen?" he asked, eyeing Hank, who was still chewing on his toy bone.

"Not this weekend. But we get a crowd every Saturday and Sunday, and sometimes it takes a while to find an ideal match. That's the most important part of the process—that the match be just right, for the pet and the adoptive family."

He nodded. "Is there a match for an eight-year-old girl whose requirements are 'super cute, snuggly and won't destroy a prized stuffed animal collection'?"

Claire laughed. "Follow me. I think I know just the pup." She led him down the row of kennels to the end. A puppy was spinning circles in the kennel, chasing her tail and letting out loud yips.

"My ears," Matt said with a smile. The puppy sure ticked off the "adorable" requirement. A springer spaniel mix, according to the chart, five months old, she was chestnut-brown and white with long, ruffled, floppy ears. Ellie would go nuts over her.

"Yeah, that's why she's still here. She yipped for twenty minutes straight at both adoption events. Including every time someone came near her kennel. She's only been here a few days, though. Another volunteer and I have been working with her a bit. She just needs some training. She's very sweet."

And loud, Matt thought. *And...active.* "Does she ever actually catch her tail and stop spinning?"

Claire laughed again. "Yes. Peanut butter treats get her to do anything."

"Would she be right for Ellie?" he asked. "My sister likes calm and orderly. I think she wants an old dog in a puppy's body."

"Well, it's important to match temperaments, and puppies can be trained, but puppies are puppies—little kids. They make noise, they're super active, they eat shoes."

"Ellie never ate a shoe, far as I know."

She laughed and touched his arm, the most casual gesture, but the feel of her fingers on his skin sent a lightning bolt through him. Standing here with her, her hand on him, it was as if they'd never broken up. Claire and Matt, high school sweethearts, married with four kids, four dogs, four cats—that's how many Claire had said she wanted of each. Plus a parrot and lovebirds. And a box turtle. He could go on.

Sometimes, over the years, late at night, Matt would berate himself for breaking up with Claire after graduation. He'd told her he needed to be focused on being the best soldier he could be, leaving it at that, and the pain on Claire's face had almost made him tell her the truth. That he wasn't and had never been and never would be good enough for her, that he'd hold her back, keep studious, bookish, intelligent Claire from fulfilling her big dreams of leaving Spring Forest for the big city. Matt wasn't a big city guy, and he'd planned to be career-army. Now, he didn't know what he was. Too many rough tours of duty, first as a soldier, then as a mechanic on dangerous missions, had left him…broken.

And here in Spring Forest, he didn't recognize himself or belong.

Focus on the mission, not yourself, he ordered himself. "I think my sister wants a temperament like Dempsey's," Matt said, gesturing at Claire's foster dog. The pooch was sitting, hadn't made a peep and didn't react in the slightest to the commotion around her.

"Dempsey is the best," Claire said. "A couple months ago, she was found chained outside an abandoned house. I don't think she ever had a home before I took her in, so

I've worked hard at acclimating her to the good life—which means passing muster on housetraining, manners, obedience, the whole thing. Now she's ready for a home, but she keeps getting passed over."

She knelt down beside the boxer and gave her a double scratch on the sides of her neck, then a kiss on her brown snout. Claire shook her head and stood up, her gaze on the dog.

He might not know Claire anymore, but a stranger could tell how much she loved that dog.

"Can't you adopt her?" he asked.

"I always want to adopt every dog I foster, but that's not my calling here," she explained. "Fostering is about preparing dogs for adoption so they can find homes. If I adopted every dog I fostered, I'd have over twenty at this point. Plus, every time a dog I work with finds a home, I can foster a new pooch."

"Must be hard to let them go," he said. "Don't you get attached?"

"Definitely," she said. "But because we do such a good job of matching furbabies and adoptive parents, I know they're going to a great home. I do worry about how attached I am to Dempsey, though. I can't explain it, but we definitely have a special bond." She gave the boxer mix another scratch on the head, and the dog looked up at her with such trust in her eyes, even Matt's battered heart was touched. "Oftentimes, that bond is there right away."

"I had no idea about any of this," he said. "There's more involved in choosing a dog than I realized. Can you help me find the right puppy for Ellie?"

"Of course," she said. "There are a few other puppies here that Ellie might like, but they all need some training. Maybe you can bring Ellie back with you and we can see who she bonds with. Furever Paws is in the process of finding a new director, so I'm helping with just about everything, from meet and greets to training to fostering to cleaning out kennels."

He glanced around the kennel area of the shelter, which had a warm, welcoming vibe to it. "It's great of you to give your time," he said. "When should I bring my niece in tomorrow?"

"I'm done teaching at the middle school at three, so I usually arrive at three thirty."

So she *had* become a teacher. That had always been her dream. But back in high school she'd wanted to leave Spring Forest and see the world, teaching her way through it. Maybe she had, for all he knew. "Works for Ellie too," he said. "See you tomorrow, then."

For a second they just looked at each other, neither making a move to leave. He wished he could pull her into his arms and hug her, hold her tight, tell her how good it was to see her, to hear her voice, to talk to her. He'd missed her so much and hadn't even known it. Which was probably a good thing. He had nothing to offer her.

As he gave Dempsey a pat and turned to walk away, he couldn't quite figure out how he could be so relieved to be leaving and so looking forward to coming back.

He paused in front of Hank's kennel. *Life is complicated, huh, boy?*

Hank tilted his head, and Matt took that as a nod.

To catch her breath and decompress, Claire took Dempsey into the fenced yard, which was thankfully empty of other volunteers. She let Dempsey off leash and for a few moments watched the dog run around the grass, sniffing and wagging her tail.

Matt Fielding. Everyone always said you never forgot your first love, and that had been very true for Claire. She'd truly believed he would be the man she'd marry and spend the rest of her life with. And then boom— a few days after a magical prom night, he'd broken up with her.

Her first boyfriend in college had proposed, and maybe the promised security had had something to do with why she'd said yes when she hadn't loved him the way she'd loved Matt. To this day, she didn't know if that had contributed to her divorce, but five years into her marriage, she'd found out that her ex-husband was cheating and in love with someone else. Now, she was living in the house they'd built out in the Kingdom Creek development, without the husband or the kids they'd talked about or the dogs they were going to adopt.

The craziest thing was that, just last week, her sister had said that Claire's problem was that she'd never gotten over Matt, and to do so she'd need to find a guy who looked like him. Tall and muscular, with those blue eyes, Matt was so good-looking and so…hot that few men in town even came close to resembling him. But apparently her sister had found someone who fit the bill, and had arranged a double date for tonight.

Half of her wanted to cancel. The other half thought she'd better protect herself against Matt's being back by going out on this date, even if her heart wouldn't be in it. Claire wanted a relationship—she wanted love and to find the man she'd spend forever with. She wanted a child—children, hopefully—and at thirty-five, she wasn't exactly a spring chicken.

"How did everything get so topsy-turvy, Demps?" she asked the dog, who'd come over with a half-eaten tennis ball. "I know you know all about that," she added, throwing the ball. Dempsey, in all her fast, muscular glory, chased after it, leaping through the air like a deer.

There was nothing like watching dogs at play to make Claire feel better and forget about her love life— the old, the nonexistent and the upcoming. She smiled as Dempsey dropped the ball at her feet. She threw it a few more times, then left the dog in the yard to play while she went to help clean the kennels that were now empty due to the lucky pups that had been adopted today.

As she reentered the shelter, she saw Birdie and Bunny Whitaker in their waterproof aprons, hard at work with the disinfectant and hose. Claire adored the sixty-something sisters—no-nonsense Birdie and dreamer Bunny—who lived together in the lovely farmhouse on Whitaker Acres, the same property the shelter was on. Opening Furever Paws had been a longtime dream of the Whitaker sisters ever since people had begun abandoning animals on Whitaker land, a pocket of rural country in what had become urban sprawl. At first they'd started an animal refuge, but when it became too much for them to handle financially, they filed for nonprofit status and started the Furever Paws Animal Rescue almost twenty years ago. Aside from the shelter with dogs and cats, the sisters kept goats, pigs, geese and even a pair of llamas on the property. They opened up Whitaker Acres to the public a few times a year so that visitors could enjoy the land and animals. Kids loved the place.

As Claire cleaned Snowball's kennel—the white shepherd-Lab mix had been adopted this morning and immediately renamed Hermione—she was glad the shelter could take in more strays and drop-offs. Furever Paws had room for about a dozen each of dogs and cats, and twice that many were cared for in foster homes, like Dempsey.

"I'll miss that adorable Snowball," Birdie said, hosing down the kennel across the way. "For twenty years I've been telling myself not to get attached to our animals." She shook her head. "Old fool." Tall and strong, her short silver hair gleaming in the afternoon sunlight, Birdie grabbed the mop, dunked it in the cleaning solution and went at the floor of the kennel until it met her satisfaction.

"I already miss Annie Jo," Bunny said, taking out the bed, blanket and toys in the next kennel and stuffing them in the huge laundry bin. Bunny looked a lot like Birdie but was shorter and plumper, her silver curls soft against her sweet face. "I love what her family renamed her—Peaches. Back in the day, a beau called me that," she added, wiggling her hips.

Claire smiled. The shelter always named the strays and those left on the doorstep. Every now and then, adopters kept the shelter names—most recently a cat named Princess Leia, who'd been there for months. Birdie and Bunny loved naming the incoming animals, and whenever they couldn't come up with a name, they held a meeting with the staff—the full-time employees, such as the shelter director, foster director and vet technician—and the volunteers, like Claire.

"Who was that very handsome man here a little while ago?" Bunny asked with a sly smile as she started sweeping out the kennel, reaching over for a stray piece of kibble that Annie Jo—Peaches—had missed. "My, he was nice to look at."

"I'm surprised you didn't rush over to ask how you could help him," Birdie said to her starry-eyed sister, wringing out the mop in the big bucket.

"Well, I *would* have," Bunny said, "but I saw Claire come back in with Dempsey and decided to leave him for her. Trust me, if I were even *ten* years younger…"

Claire laughed as Birdie shook her head again, her trademark move. Neither Whitaker sister had ever married, though Claire did know that Bunny had been engaged in her early twenties until her fiancé had tragically died. Birdie never talked about her love life, and though Claire had tried a time or two to get Bunny to spill about Birdie's romantic life, the sisters were clearly loyal to each other's secrets. As they should be.

But no matter how much or how little experience the Whitaker sisters had in the romance department, they were both wise—Birdie in common sense and Bunny in keeping an open mind and heart. Talking to the two always set Claire straight, or at least made her feel better.

Which was why she was going to be honest right now.

"That was the guy who broke my heart into a million pieces after high school graduation," she said. "Matt Fielding. I cried for six months straight."

"And then married the first guy who asked you out," Birdie said with an *uh-huh* look on her face.

"Yup," Claire said, spraying disinfectant on the bars of the last kennel and wiping them down with a clean rag. "But there's hope for me. Guess who has a blind date tonight? My sister and her husband set me up."

"Ooh," Bunny said, her blue eyes twinkling. "How exciting. To me, blind dates are synonymous with 'you never know.' Could be the man of your dreams."

Birdie wrinkled up her face. "Blind dates are usually the pits." She glanced at Claire, instantly contrite, then threw her arms up in the air. "Oh, come on. They are."

Claire laughed. "Well, if the date takes my mind off the fact that my first love is back in town? Mission accomplished."

"Oh boy," Birdie said, pausing the mop. "Someone is still very hung up on her first love."

"Oh dear," Bunny agreed.

And before Claire could say that *of course* she was—*you did see him, after all*—that cute little springer spaniel she'd shown Matt started howling up a storm.

"Someone wants her dinner *now*," Bunny said with a laugh.

"I'm on feeding duty for the dogs," Claire said, putting the disinfectant back on the supplies shelf and the rag in Bunny's laundry basket. "If I don't see you two before I leave for the day, congrats on a great Sunday. Five adult dogs adopted plus the puppies and cats."

"It was a good day," Bunny said. "Good luck on that date tonight."

Claire smiled. "Who knows? Maybe he *will* be the man of my dreams."

She was putting on a brave front for the sisters—not that she needed to, since she could always be honest with them. But sometimes Claire reverted to that old need to save face, to not seem like she cared quite so much that she was single, when she wanted to be partnered, to find that special someone to share her life with, to build a life with. She loved Dempsey to pieces, but most nights, unless she had book club or a social event like someone else's engagement party or birthday, it was her and the boxer mix snuggled on the sofa in her living room, watching *Dancing with the Stars* or a Netflix movie, a rawhide chew for Dempsey and a single-serve bag of microwave popcorn for her.

There was room on that couch for a man.

But in any case, Matt Fielding was not the man of her dreams, whether she was "hung up or him" or not. Seventeen-year-old Claire had been madly in love. Now, she was a thirty-five-year-old divorced woman staring down her biological clock. "Man of her dreams" was silly nonsense. Hadn't the supposed man of her dreams dumped her almost two decades ago as if she'd meant nothing? Ha, like that was part of the dream?

Matt Fielding was not the man of her dreams.

If she said it enough, she might believe it.

And if there was no such thing, then what *was* she looking for in a partner?

She'd never put much stock in checklists, since she could rattle off a list of adjectives, like *kind*, and non-negotiables, like *doesn't rip apart his exes or his mother on the date*, but everything came down to chemistry. How you felt with someone. How someone made you feel. If your head and heart were engaged. She'd never experienced chemistry the way she had with Matt Fielding. But her motto ever since she'd started volunteering for Furever Paws was: Everything is possible. The most timid dog, the hissiest cat, could become someone's dearest treasure. *Everything is possible.* Including Claire finding love again. At thirty-five.

She peeled off her waterproof gloves and tossed them in the used-gloves bin, then headed toward the door to start filling bowls with kibble and sneaking in medicines where needed.

"Oh, Claire," Birdie said. "Some advice. In the first five minutes, ask your date if he likes dogs. If he says no, you'll know he's not for you."

Bunny tilted her head. "Now, Birdie. Not everyone loves animals like we do."

Apparently, the entire Whitaker family loved animals to the point that all their nicknames were inspired by animals. Birdie's real name was Bernadette. Bunny's was Gwendolyn. There was a Moose—Doug—who'd sadly died long ago. And a Gator, aka Greg, who advised the sisters on financial matters.

"The man of Claire's dreams will love dogs," Birdie said. "That's nonnegotiable. If her blind date says dogs slobber and bark and are a pain in the neck, she can tune him out the rest of the night."

Claire smiled. As usual, Birdie Whitaker was right.

Chapter Two

Matt held his niece's hand as they entered the Main Street Grille later that night, the smell of burgers and fish and chips reminding him how hungry he was. His sister, Laura, and her husband, Kurt, had insisted on taking him out to dinner to celebrate his homecoming.

"His home*staying*!" Ellie had said, squeezing him into one of her famous hugs.

He adored the eight-year-old. He barely knew her— had rarely seen her since she'd been born because of his tours—but the moment he'd arrived yesterday, she'd latched on to him like he was the fun, exciting uncle she'd missed out on, and of course, he couldn't let her down. He'd played soccer with her. He'd read her two bedtime stories last night, then she'd read him one, and he'd almost fallen asleep right there in her pink-and-

purple room. This morning, he'd played Hiker Barbie
with her in the backyard, his Barbie falling into a ra-
vine, and her Barbie saving her with her search-and-
rescue skills and the help of Barbie's golden retriever,
Tanner. She'd spent a good hour talking to Matt about
dogs, after she'd instructed Tanner to grab his Barbie's
jeans cuff and pull her up to safety. The girl was dog-
crazy. And he was Ellie-crazy. He was determined to
help her find just the right pooch to love.

With Claire Asher's help. Amazing.

"We love this restaurant," Laura said as the hostess
led them through the dimly lit space to a table for four
near a window. "During the day, it's more of a diner, but
at night it transforms into a pub. Apparently, it's quite
the nostalgic place to get engaged."

Matt glanced around the restaurant. There were quite
a few obvious dates.

And, oh hell, was that *Claire*?

On an obvious date.

He turned away so that his staring wouldn't draw her
attention. Then, as he sat down, he took another glance.
Dammit. Yes, it was. Four tables away, diagonally. She
was sitting with her own sister, Della, and two men were
across from them. The one across from Claire looked
slick. He had gelled hair and trendy eyeglasses and was
holding court, making Claire laugh.

Crud. He used to make Claire Asher laugh.

At least she's happy, he told himself.

"What are you having, Uncle Matt?" Ellie asked.
"I'm getting the mac and cheese. No, the cowabunga

burger. No, the mac and cheese. Or should I have the spaghetti and meatballs?"

He focused his attention on his niece. The poor thing had an incredibly crooked strawberry-blond braid with weird tufts sticking out. Ellie had asked him to do the honors for tonight's "special dinner," and Laura had given the tutorial as he went. When he was done, his sister had had to leave the room to keep herself from bursting into laughter. But Ellie, checking out his handi-work with a hand mirror and her back to the hall mirror, declared her braid *just perfect!*

"Well, I know your favorite is mac and cheese," he said, "and since this is a special night, I think you should get your favorite." Matt forced himself to look at the menu and not Claire.

But she looked so damned pretty. The candle on the table just slightly illuminated her. She'd dolled up a bit since her shift at the shelter. Her pink-red lips were glossy, and her light blond hair was sleek to her shoul-ders. She wore an off-white V-neck sweater, and a deli-cate gold chain around her neck.

"That's right," his sister said, smiling at Ellie. "This is a special night—celebrating Uncle Matt's long-awaited homecoming."

"Homestaying!" Ellie said with a grin.

That got his attention. Because *was* this something to celebrate? Thirty-six and living in his sister's guest room? No clue where he was headed, what he'd do. Visiting his family while he figured things out made sense, he reminded himself. He had ideas, of course. And skills. But he felt wrong in his skin, suddenly adrift in this different life.

You're an American hero and don't you forget it, his sister had said when he'd mentioned that earlier. *You'll adapt and build a new life—hopefully here in town.*

With Claire Asher to run into everywhere he went? No, sir. He was two for two on his first full day in Spring Forest. He couldn't do that to himself on a daily basis. But until he decided where to go and what to do, Spring Forest, it was.

He took one more look at Claire out the side of his menu. *Oh please.* Her date was offering her a bite of something. As Claire smiled and leaned forward to accept the fork—with her hand, thank God, and not with those luscious lips—Matt felt his gut tighten and his appetite disappear.

He'd help Ellie find her dog. Which meant seeing Claire one more time tomorrow. And then maybe he'd leave town. There was no way he could figure out what the hell he was going to do with his life if he was going to constantly run into her—and be unable to stop thinking about her.

Dammit.

Now she was laughing at something Slick had said. Great. Tonight was a *real* celebration.

Claire's date liked dogs. Loved them, in fact. He—Andrew, thirty-five, divorced, two children of whom he shared joint custody—even had a dog, a yellow Lab named Sully.

And Andrew was very attractive. Her sister hadn't been kidding about him looking like Matt, to a degree. They had the same coloring, the dark hair—though Matt's was more military-short—the blue eyes, the strong nose and square jawline, both men managing to look both refined and rugged at the same time. Andrew was in a suit and tie, but Claire had seen Matt Fielding in a suit only once—on prom night, the black tuxedo he'd paired with a skinny white silk tie and black Converse high-tops. That night, she'd thought there was nothing sexier on the planet than her boyfriend.

Her date for tonight was charming and kind and attentive, asking all kinds of questions about her job as a teacher. He showed her photos of his kids and beamed with pride about them, which Claire found sweet and touching. Over the past few years, when she'd started worrying that she wouldn't find Mr. Right-Part-Two, she'd thought about marrying a man with kids and becoming a great stepmother. And there was adoption, of course. Her single friend Sally had adopted a little girl from foster care, and though there were challenges, she'd never seen her friend so happy, so fulfilled.

Another of Claire's mottoes over the past few years had been: If you want to find your life partner, if you want to have a child, however that child may come into your life, you have to keep your mind and heart open.

And now here was seemingly perfect Andrew. Even clear-eyed, hard-nosed Birdie Whitaker would be impressed by him and the prospects of a second date. She could just hear romantic Bunny running down how things would go: *And then a* third *date at that revolving restaurant on the zillionth floor in the fancy hotel in Raleigh. Then amazing sex in your suite for the night. Then exclusivity. Then a proposal on your six-month-iversary. You'll be married to a wonderful man and have stepchildren to dote on and love by summer—you could be a June bride if you're only engaged four months!* Oh God, sometimes Claire thought it would be wonderful to be Bunny.

Problem was, though, that despite how wonderful Andrew seemed, Claire felt zero chemistry. Zero pull. The thought of getting to know him better didn't really interest her. The idea of kissing him left her cold.

No fair! And she knew exactly why this man who loved dogs, who'd even showed her a slew of photos of handsome Sully on his phone, wasn't having any effect on any part of her at all.

Because for the past few hours, as she'd been getting ready for the date, Matt had been on her mind. How could he not be? She hadn't seen him in almost twenty years and then, whammo, there he was today, at her sanctuary, the place where she always felt at home, at peace. Matt Fielding suddenly kneeling in front of a dog's kennel at Furever Paws. Unbelievable.

She'd started out the evening thinking she would not let being all verklempt at seeing her first love derail this date. And so she'd put a little more effort than she otherwise might have into her hair and makeup and outfit, as if trying to force herself to give the date a real shot instead of knowing her heart just wouldn't be in it.

And now, as Andrew signaled their waiter for their check, which he insisted on paying for the table, all she wanted was to be back home, sipping this excellent chardonnay in a hot bath to soothe her muscles after the long day at the shelter. And to deal with being flooded by memories of Matt. The first time they'd met. Kissed. When he'd opened up about his older brother, who hadn't come home from Afghanistan. His parents' pride and worry that Matt had enlisted in his brother's honor. That they may lose another son. Matt had promised his mother he'd email every night to say good-night, to let her know he was okay. And he had for years; his sister, Laura, had shared that with her when they'd run into each other a few years back.

Matt had ended up outliving his parents, and when Laura had let Claire know when they'd run into each other another time, she'd said that Matt got through it only because he wouldn't have to worry about shattering their hearts a second time, after all.

All these memories had come rushing back while she'd been applying mascara and stepping into a gentle spray of Chanel N° 19. Her date with Andrew Haverman, attorney-at-law, never stood a chance.

Claire shook her head at herself.

"So, I hope we can go for a drink," Andrew said as he signed the credit card slip. He slid a hopeful, very-interested smile at Claire.

Claire's sister stood up, prompting her husband to do the same. "We have to get up pretty early tomorrow. You two go, though," she added with her own hopeful smile, glancing from Claire to Andrew and back to Claire.

Don't you dare mess this up! Claire could hear Della shouting telepathically to her. *Get Matt Fielding out of your head this instant! I know you! GET. HIM. OUT! Andrew has a dog named Sully!*

Despite the dog, despite everything, she couldn't get Matt out of her head. As her date was pocketing his shiny gold credit card and receipt, she glanced around the restaurant, trying to think of an excuse. She didn't want to go for a drink, extend the date. She didn't want to see this man again, despite, despite, despite. Avoiding her sister's narrowed stare, Claire kept looking around the restaurant, sending a smile to a former student at a table with her parents, another smile to a couple who'd adopted two kittens from Furever Paws a few weeks ago—and then her smile froze.

Claire felt her eyes widen as her gaze was caught on a very crooked strawberry-blond braid halfway down a little girl's back. She'd seen a similarly hued braid—though a very tidy one—on Matt's niece when she'd run into his sister and the girl a couple of months ago in the supermarket.

Oh God. Don't let me look next to her and see Matt.

But there he was. Now staring at her. Glaring at her, actually.

Whoa there, guy.

But suddenly her date was standing up too, and so she had to. Her group would walk right past Matt's table. There was no way she couldn't say hello, if not to Matt, then to his sister.

Awk-ward.

"You've *got* to be kidding me," Claire's sister hiss-whispered in her ear as they headed toward the door—toward Matt's table. "No wonder you've been so distracted!"

"Actually, I just noticed him a few seconds ago," Claire admitted. If she'd known he was there this whole time, she would have excused herself to the restroom to hyperventilate.

"Claire!" Matt's sister said with a surprised smile as they were about to pass.

Oh hell. Claire paused as her group moved on to the waiting area, collecting their coats from the racks. Her sister was furiously gesturing her over by tipping her head to the side, her mouth in a comical grimace.

"I hear I owe you a big thank-you, Claire!" Laura was saying. She sat across from Matt and next to her husband. "Matt mentioned he ran into you at Furever Paws and that you're going to help Ellie choose a puppy tomorrow."

Claire glanced at Matt, who was now sitting with a total lack of expression on his handsome face. Better than the glare? Not really.

"I'm so excited, I'm going to explode," Ellie said, her hazel eyes shining. "Thank you for helping me! I can't wait to see the puppies!"

Aww. Ellie was adorable and sweet. "My pleasure," Claire said.

"Just remember the rules, Matt and Ellie," Laura said, raising an eyebrow between the two. "House-trained is a must. And the puppy must know basic commands before he walks into our home. Oh—and no bigger than medium-sized when fully grown."

Uh-oh, Claire thought. She'd have her work cut out for her there. Did any of the puppies fit the bill? Certainly not the springer spaniel, who'd peed right on Claire's foot this morning while she'd been fluffing her blanket. Though she *was* expected to be medium-sized. And the three other contenders were housetrained, but two would be huge, and a consistent "sit" was still beyond all of them, in spite of lots of training with high-value treats.

"Your date is waiting for you," Matt practically growled, gesturing toward the door.

Her sister was still furiously head-gesturing for Claire to get the hell away from Matt Fielding and join the present and possible future—not be stuck in the past.

Awk-ward, she thought again as she smiled at everyone and dashed toward her group.

But as her date held the door open for her, she dared a glance back at Matt.

And he was looking right at her, his expression more readable now. He was angry-jealous!

He'd dumped her, remember? To live his own life on his terms.

"So, that nightcap?" her date asked, helping her into her coat.

Do not look over at Matt, she ordered herself, aware that he had to be watching right then.

"To be honest, I just saw a ghost," she said, surprising herself with her candor. "I think I'd like to just call it a night."

Her sister rolled her eyes and shook her head so imperceptibly that likely only Claire caught it.

Her date looked confused.

"An ex," her brother-in-law explained to Andrew.

"Ah. I get it," Andrew said. "Happened to me just last night while on another blind date, and crazy as it was, I ended up with the ex for the rest of the night." A salacious expression lit his face. "One-time thing," he rushed to say, seeming to realize he'd said too much.

At least Claire wouldn't have to feel too bad about ditching him.

As they headed to her sister's SUV, she could still see Matt's face so clearly in her mind. How could she not be over him? How? Eighteen years later?

He was coming to the shelter tomorrow. She'd see him again. He had a purpose and so did she, and then he'd leave and that would be that.

Yeah, right.

Corporal McCabbers was telling Matt about his girlfriend back home; Penny was her name, with long red hair and green eyes. He and McCabbers sat in the back of the vehicle, headed for a broken-down US Army truck that they had to get running pronto.

Ten more days and I'm home, McCabbers was saying, and Matt envied his buddy's ability to lose himself in his memories and hopes for the future—because his woman was still his woman. Matt had a string of hookups and failed off-base, short-term relationships. There'd been women over the years, but Claire Asher's face was always the one he saw in his dreams, his fantasies.

And home? There'd been no home for almost two decades. Home was wherever Matt was.

"There's the truck," he heard the driver call.

He and McCabbers waited for their vehicle to stop, for the all-clear from the driver to duck out toward the truck under cover of night.

No sooner had their boots hit the dry, dusty ground

than a burst of flame erupted before Matt's eyes, the explosion throwing him back hard.

The pain in his left leg was unlike anything he'd felt before. "Fielding!" he heard McCabbers shouting. "Fielding!" And then he'd felt nothing at all.

Matt bolted up, a trickle of sweat running down his chest, his breath ragged and coming hard. He glanced around, and then closed his eyes.

He was home. His sister's house.

Letting out a breath, he dropped back down on the soft sheets and pulled the comforter up to his chest.

He didn't have the nightmares as often as he used to. In rehab, where he'd woken up after being unconscious for two days, he'd had the dreams every time he'd fallen asleep. But as his wounds healed and his leg strengthened, the nightmares had lessened. The memories remained though.

He could still picture dragging himself over to McCabbers and tying his shirt around the wound in his buddy's leg, which had looked a hell of a lot worse than Matt's own. The driver of their vehicle had been able to get back to them, dragging him and McCabbers into the truck and booking it out of there, saving their lives. McCabbers had gone on to marry his girlfriend six months later in Las Vegas, on one crutch but otherwise alive and well.

Matt had a hell of a lot to be grateful for. And Claire Asher deserved to be happy. Wasn't that why he'd broken up with her all those years ago? So she could have a better life than the one he'd be able to share with her?

Still, he couldn't stop speculating about how Claire's

evening had progressed. If it had progressed. If she'd invited Slick home. If he was still there.

None of your business, he reminded himself. Help your niece find the perfect puppy, then pack up and find a place where you belong.

Chapter Three

"That very good-looking man and a little girl are out front," Bunny whispered with a smile as Claire came in the back door of Furever Paws on Monday afternoon. Claire returned Sunshine to her kennel and secured the door, noting the time of the walk on the big whiteboard on the wall. The year-old rottie mix had been at the kennel for two days, and was slowly warming up to walking on a leash. "Says he's here to see Claire Asher about adopting a puppy." Bunny smiled slyly.

Claire shook her head at Bunny's expression. "Well, he is."

"I can't wait to hear about your date," Bunny said, her blue eyes twinkling. "Find me later and tell me everything."

Do I want to be reminded of any of it? No. "There's

nothing really to tell. No chemistry, even if he was great on paper."

Bunny nodded. "I get it. A blind date, no matter if he's Pierce Brosnan, can't compete with a first love on the brain."

Especially when that first love is in the same restaurant.

Claire glanced at the clock. It was exactly three thirty. She'd practically raced here after finishing up at school, grateful that her last period of the day was monitoring a study hall. She'd wanted to get to the shelter with some time to spare before Matt arrived so that she wouldn't be flustered. So, she'd taken Sunshine out, grounded herself on her turf and was ready by the time she got back inside.

Claire left the dog kennels and headed to the main lobby. She almost sucked in her breath at the sight of Matt, looking as good as Bunny had noted. He wore a navy-blue Henley, a black leather jacket and dark jeans.

She gave him a fast smile, then turned her focus on Ellie, who was practically jumping in place.

"Hi, Miss Claire!" Ellie said with a huge grin on her adorable face. "I can't wait to see the puppies! Can you believe my mom finally said okay to me having a dog? I've been waiting years!"

"Well, you *are* only eight," Matt pointed out, giving her still-crooked braid a playful pull.

"I've wanted a dog since I was two," Ellie said. "But I had to show my mom I could take care of a dog. And I can! And I will!"

Her handsome uncle smiled. "I know it."

"Well, to the kennels, then," Claire said, leading the way. This was good. They were both ignoring running into each other last night. "We have four puppies and three dogs between a year and a half and two—they've got a lot of puppy in them too. Let's start with the puppies and see who you like."

She glanced at Matt, who was quiet.

"Just one rule," Claire added to the girl. "No putting your fingers in the kennels. Some dogs might nip because they're a little nervous or need more training time."

At Ellie's serious nod, Claire stopped in front of a six-month-old shepherd mix, Tabitha, whose amber eyes darted over at them. She stood and barked up a storm, sending the other dogs into a commotion, and ambled over to the bars of the kennel. She sniffed the air for a treat and when one wasn't forthcoming, she padded back over to her bed and began chewing on her rope toy. Tabitha had an ear infection that required medication for the next week, and the irritation might have been making her act out a bit.

"She's really cute," Ellie said with a bit of a frown. She knelt down in front of the cage. "Hi, puppy. I'm Ellie."

The puppy barked like crazy again and came over and sniffed the air again, then went back to her bed.

Ellie tilted her head and bit her lip. Claire could immediately tell the girl didn't feel a connection with Tabitha.

"And next we have a five-month-old springer spaniel puppy," Claire said, moving to the spinning pooch in the next kennel. In true form, Belle began spinning in circles, trying to chase her tail.

Ellie gasped. She dropped down on her knees in front of the kennel, watching the puppy with delight on her face. "Hi, there! Hi, puppy!"

The puppy stopped spinning and came closer to Ellie.

"Remember, sweetheart, don't put your fingers in the kennel," Matt said, and Claire nodded at him.

Belle barked, excitedly wagging her tail, jumping up at the kennel door and trying to sniff Ellie. She sat down and barked at Ellie, then made a play bow.

"She wants to play with me!" Ellie said. "You are so adorable!" she added. "You're exactly what I dreamed about!"

Belle began barking like crazy and spinning around, desperately trying to catch her tail in her mouth.

Claire widened her eyes and looked at Matt, who was grimacing.

Ellie laughed, her entire face lit up with happiness. "I see your name is Belle, and I know that means beautiful, and you are, but I think you look more like a Sparkle. That's what I'd name you, Sparkle." She bolted up. "This is the one! This is my puppy!"

Claire couldn't remember the last time she saw someone so excited, and she saw excited kids a lot during the course of adoptions.

"Yup, you're the one, Sparkle!" Ellie said, dropping down to her knees again and smiling at the puppy.

Who squatted and peed right on the floor, the mess seeping into the corridor to the point that they all jumped back.

"Oops," Ellie said. Then she seemed to remember what her mom said about housetraining, and worry slid into her expression. Her shoulders slumped, and her face scrunched up for a moment. Claire could tell the girl was trying not to cry.

"Well, Sparkle is definitely not housetrained," Matt said gently, a hand on his niece's shoulder. "And she sure is noisy and busy. Why don't we—"

"I'll clean it up!" Ellie added, looking from her uncle to Claire, and back at the puppy, and then back at Claire. "Are there paper towels or something?"

Claire smiled and got the roll of heavy-duty brown paper towels. "I'll take care of it, honey." She quickly mopped up the mess.

"Your mom made her requirements very clear, sweets," Matt said. "So even though Sparkle is cute, she's a long way from being trained and she seems kind of hyper."

Ellie's little shoulders slumped again, and she sucked in a breath.

Aww. This was always a difficult thing, when someone fell for an animal that wasn't the right fit for the home. "Ellie," Claire said, "two kennels down is an adorable chiweenie named Tucker who's housetrained and knows basic commands. A chiweenie is a cross between a Chihuahua and a dachshund. He'll be small even when fully grown, so he's a great size for a kid."

Ellie followed Claire to Tucker's kennel, her head hung low. "I've never heard of a chiweenie before." But there was no excitement in her voice.

"Meet Tucker," Claire said, gesturing at the little

dog, who was as calm as could be. He lay on his bed, gnawing on a rope toy. He was very cute, with floppy, cinnamon-colored ears and a long snout, and tended to look like he was smiling.

Ellie gave him something of a smile. "Hi, Tucker. You seem nice."

Tucker didn't even glance up.

"He can be slow to warm up to people," Claire explained.

But Ellie raced back to Sparkle's kennel and knelt in front of it. "I wish I could take you home, Sparkle." She sat there and watched the dog chasing her tail.

Claire looked at Matt, whose expression matched his niece's. This couldn't be easy, and she probably should have thought to warn him that something like this could happen. She'd been a little too shocked yesterday when she'd seen him at the shelter to even form an extra thought. And last night at the restaurant, all rational thought had *poofed* from her head.

"Well, let's look at the other pups," Matt said, reaching his hand toward Ellie. He glanced at Claire. "I'll bet there's another puppy that Ellie will fall in love with."

"Definitely," Claire said. "Because guess who's next, Ellie? A super sweet year-old shepherd mix named Dumpling. I'll bet you'll like him. He's super snuggly." He was inconsistent on commands, but he did know *stay*. He was slated to be on the large side of medium, which might be stretching it. Sometimes it was impossible to really know how big a dog would get.

"I guess I can meet him." But Ellie didn't get up from where she sat in front of Belle's cage. And even from here, Claire could see the glistening of Ellie's eyes. The girl was trying hard not to cry.

"Honey, maybe we could come back next weekend for the adoption event," Matt said. "These puppies will have had an extra week of training, and you might just fall in love with a dog you barely noticed this time."

"Okay, Uncle Matt," Ellie said, but she still didn't stand up. "It's okay, Sparkle. You'll find someone to love you, and you'll be best friends. That's what my mom tells me when I'm sad about not having a best friend."

Claire held her breath and glanced at Matt, whose broad shoulders slumped.

"As long as I'm nice and friendly, I'm doing my best," Ellie said to the puppy. "Then one day I'll make a best friend. It can happen anytime, Mommy said."

Claire swallowed.

Ellie let out a little sigh. "You'd be a great best friend, Sparkle. But maybe another girl will come here today, and you'll get to go home with her. Just be nice and friendly, okay, Sparkle?"

Oh God.

Ellie stood, tears shimmering in her eyes. "Bye, Sparkle. I love you."

Claire looked at Matt. He looked like he might cry too. And she'd seen him cry. Just once, a long, long time ago when he lost his brother.

Matt cleared his throat. "Tucker might be just right for you, once he gets to know you," he said, kneeling down to be eye level with his niece. "Then you get to say *chiweenie* a lot. 'I'm taking my chiweenie out. Chi-weenie, where are you?'"

"I guess," Ellie said. She started to follow Matt toward Tucker's kennel next door. "Uncle Matt?" she asked, stopping. "I know Sparkle isn't housetrained like Mommy wants, but I could housetrain her. I've read all about how."

Matt seemed to consider that. "Well, let me send your mom a picture of her." He took out his cell phone and snapped a photo. "Ooh, that's a good one. I'll let her know Sparkle doesn't exactly meet the requirements, but that we're both willing to work extra hard training her." He texted something and then waited.

Claire was hoping Laura would be unable to resist the puppy's adorableness.

His phone pinged. "'Not housetrained?'" he read aloud. "'Doesn't know a single command? I'm sorry, Matt. No.'" He turned to Ellie. "Sweetie, you'll be at school from the time you leave at seven thirty until you get home at three," Matt said gently. "That's all day. That would put everything to do with caring for Sparkle on your mom's shoulders."

"Yeah," Ellie whispered, and her face scrunched up again. Claire knew the girl was willing herself not to cry.

"Could we put a hold on Belle—Sparkle?" Matt asked. "Just until we can talk to my sister face-to-face? Maybe she'll compromise on a requirement."

"But not both," Ellie said, her face crumpling again. "Sparkle isn't housetrained. She doesn't know any commands."

Claire's heart was so heavy, her knees might not hold

her up much longer. "I'll put a hold until tomorrow," she assured him.

Ellie looked both hopeful and not. "Thanks for showing me the puppies, Miss Claire. Bye, Sparkle. I love you."

The little brown-and-white pup gave a little bark and then continued chasing her tail.

"She said bye back!" Ellie said, a smile breaking through.

Matt smiled and took his niece's hand. "Why did I think this would be a snap?" he whispered to Claire.

"Few things ever are," Claire said.

He held her gaze for a moment. "I'll be in touch as soon as I can."

So much for keeping her distance, cutting contact, moving on. Claire bit her lip and nodded, watching the pair walk away, Matt's arm around the little girl's dejected shoulders.

Oh, am I in trouble, she thought.

"No and no," Laura whispered after Matt made another pitch to his sister for Sparkle. They stood at the kitchen island, Matt badly chopping peppers for a salad while Laura checked the chicken roasting in the oven. The house sure smelled good. "But look at this face," he said, picking up his phone and showing her the adorable pup again.

"You're getting pepper bits on your phone," Laura said, refusing to look at the photo. "And could you cut those a little thinner?"

"Uh-oh, you're mad at me."

"Of course I am!" she said. "I explicitly said the dog had to be housetrained and know basic commands. This Sparkle is neither! And now I'm the bad guy."

"I know, and I'm sorry. But she's incredibly cute," Matt said. "And Ellie fell for her hard."

Laura sighed and put on oven mitts to take out the baked potatoes. "I just had all the area rugs cleaned, and the bedroom carpets are brand-new. I work part-time, I volunteer at Ellie's school. I can't housetrain a puppy, Matt."

Wait a minute.

Yes.

Of course!

Why hadn't this occurred to him before? "*I'll* train the puppy," he said. "I'll read a book, watch some videos. I'm sure I'll figure it out."

Laura looked at him. "Matt, honey, I appreciate that, but no. I don't want accidents in the house for weeks on end. I don't want a dog that doesn't stop or stay when I need it to. Sorry, Matt, but I'm putting my foot down."

She had every right. "Ah hell, I really screwed this up," he said. "I shouldn't have taken Ellie to see puppies she wouldn't be able to adopt."

His sister put a hand on his arm. "I'm sure that just the right puppy will come along."

"I guess," he said, hating that he'd have to disappoint his niece—and Claire.

"Thanks for helping with the salad," she said, eyeing the bowl of misshapen lettuce and oddly shaped peppers and cucumbers. She laughed, then shrugged. "I'll call it Uncle Salad."

"I'd better go call Claire and let her know to release the hold on Sparkle," he said.

Laura nodded. "I am sorry it didn't work out with this particular dog. And I do appreciate you doing the heavy lifting with the search. It's not easy being the yes or no woman."

He smiled. "I know."

"Dinner in ten minutes," she said, which meant he'd better go tell Claire now, and then Ellie.

His sister had always been no-nonsense, though when you had kids you probably had to be, or you'd end up with four untrained puppies peeing on the area rugs.

He nodded and headed up to the guest room and closed the door. Phone in hand, he sat on the bed and fished out the card Claire had given him, the shelter's information on one side, her cell phone on the back.

He punched in her number. The sound of her voice saying *hello?* sent a little tremor through him. He'd probably never get used to just calling her up, hearing her voice, running into her.

"Hi, Claire, it's Matt. You can let the hold go, unfortunately."

"I'm sorry. Is Ellie okay?"

"No. My sister's mad at me for making her the bad guy, so my brother-in-law is probably getting an earful right now and will be pissed at me too."

"Oh no," Claire said.

"I even offered to train Sparkle myself, but my sister won't go for it. I get it, but I wish this could have worked out."

"You'd be willing to train the puppy?" Claire asked.

"Sure. I mean, I know I don't have experience, but I'd do my research. It's not like I'm focused on anything else right now."

She was silent for a second, then said, "Matt, I have a crazy idea."

"I'm all ears."

"I live in the Kingdom Creek development—a house with a big fenced yard. There's a small one-bedroom apartment over the garage. Maybe you could move in temporarily to foster and train Sparkle, and when she's ready, she can be adopted by Ellie. Your niece can even help you train her."

Huh. Win-win for everyone, especially him in the short-term. He'd have his own place, even if it was connected to Claire's house. He'd have some space to figure out his future. And Claire had used the word *temporarily*, so she was making it clear he'd go when the puppy was trained.

Best of all, he had an immediate mission: to train a cute puppy for his beloved niece.

"I'll move in tomorrow," he said.

There was silence for a moment, then she rattled off the address and some information about the place. The apartment came with basic furnishings, so he'd just have to move his big duffel bag.

"Thanks, Claire," he said. "I know I'm probably not your first choice of tenant."

"At least I know you. Or did," she said. "The last couple I rented to was a disaster."

Or did. The words hit him like a left hook in the gut. "See you tomorrow," he said, needing to get off the phone, to break the connection with her.

But despite her saying goodbye and the click in his ear, an image of Claire Asher in a long, pale pink dress came storming into his mind. Prom night, so many years ago. They'd long planned to lose their virginity to each other that night as a tribute to their past and a promise for their future, but as the night went on, Matt knew he wouldn't touch her. She'd known he was going to enlist, like his brother had before him, but she kept talking about when he came home, saying that she'd wait for him, reminding him she'd be semi-local in Chapel Hill for college but that she could transfer depending on where he got stationed. But on prom night, with Claire looking like a movie star in that beautiful pink gown, the whole world open to her, all Matt could think about was smart, interesting Claire putting her life on hold when she deserved so much more.

Except she'd stayed in Spring Forest. Had gone to the local college. Married a hometown guy. Why? Why hadn't she used the opportunity of being free to spread those glittering wings of hers? He didn't understand it.

He supposed he'd have a lot of chances to ask her now that he'd be living in her house.

Chapter Four

"You *what*?" Claire's sister, Della, said as she handed Claire her sesame chicken from the Taste of China delivery bag. Della had come over to catch up on the blind date, running into Matt at the restaurant, and what-is-this-about-helping-him-and-his-niece-pick-out-a-puppy? By the time Claire got to the part about Matt moving into the "in-law apartment" to train the dog, Della was shaking her head with older sister wisdom. "You're going to be living together!"

"Hardly," Claire said, opening up the container of sesame chicken. Nothing, not even her nerves, could spoil her appetite for this deliciousness. "The apartment is completely separate with its own entrance. I'll rarely see him." She pulled apart her chopsticks and dug in.

Della narrowed her gaze and picked up a succulent

bite of beef in garlic sauce and a broccoli spear. "Except the entrance is up those deck stairs." She pointed with her chopsticks toward the sliding glass door to the back-yard, where Dempsey lay in her memory foam dog bed. "You'll see him every time you're sitting here. And con-sidering we're in your living room and your kitchen is directly in front of us, you'll be seeing him constantly."

"He *is* nice to look at," Claire said. "So that's a plus."

Della put down her chopsticks. "Honey. There isn't even a word for how badly he hurt you. You can't go through that again. *I* can't!"

Yup, Claire remembered. All her plans for herself had gone up in smoke. Maybe another girl would have rallied and gone off to the University of North Carolina in Chapel Hill, as planned. Planned—ha! Back then "the plan" had been for Matt to be in basic training, then stationed somewhere stateside or overseas, and they'd see each other when he could come home for precious and rare breaks. She'd graduate, he'd come home for good and then they'd plan what was next. Except in-stead, he'd broken up with her with barely an explana-tion, and she'd been so heartbroken and confused that the pain had messed with her head. She'd been unable to think straight, to think of anything except how her life had been derailed.

Her poor sister had tried to get her to see that it was also an opportunity, to go to school and start her new life far away. But Claire hadn't been able to pull herself up and out of her heartache. She hadn't gone away to school, hadn't gone to college at all that first semester. Instead, she'd cried constantly, unwilling to get out of bed, unwilling to imagine a future without the guy she loved—without Matt Fielding.

Her sister had come over every day, bringing her food she ate one bite of, brushing her hair, making her bed around her, and finally, after three weeks, dragging her out of bed for a sisters trip to the Bahamas, whether she wanted to go or not. Della had packed her suitcase and forced her on the plane. The white sand and turquoise water, the fruity drinks and warm, breezy air had helped restore her.

Back home, she'd finally enrolled in the local college, married her second boyfriend, a man she hadn't realized was all wrong for her. Luckily, by then, her passion for becoming a teacher, particularly of middle school kids in the throes of figuring out who they were, had gripped her. Claire had run with it, getting her master's and advising extracurricular groups. She loved teaching. By the time her marriage had fallen apart, Claire had had her own busy life, which included volunteering at Furever Paws. Or at least that was what she'd told herself to explain why her husband's betrayal hadn't steamrollered her the way it should have.

I don't believe you ever really loved me, her husband had said when he told her he'd fallen for someone else, really fallen, and that he was leaving Claire. But he was wrong; she had loved him, very much. *I think you rebounded with me after your high school sweetheart destroyed you.*

Destroyed. Heavy word. One her sister would apply, as well. But Claire hadn't been destroyed. People had to be resilient, had to move on. Still, no sense not being careful with yourself to avoid having your heart smashed to smithereens in the future.

Claire smiled and squeezed her sister's hand. "Eat up. And stop worrying. Matt Fielding and I aren't getting back together. I'm just bringing together a little girl and a puppy."

"Except Matt and said puppy are moving in upstairs."

Claire put down her bite of sesame chicken. She could lie to herself all she wanted, but she'd never been able to lie to Della, who saw through her. "Every time I see him, my heart races and my stomach flip-flops, and these little chills slide up my spine."

"Yeah, that's called not having gotten over your first boyfriend. Who broke your heart. Who's moving upstairs. Who you said has no plans—to stay or go."

Claire sobered up fast. She had to be careful about Matt.

"I'm just saying, Claire. You want what you want—a husband and child. A family. You've been saying yes to men who ask you out in the supermarket. You've been saying yes to blind dates—although, you derailed a perfectly good one, even though I suppose you might have dodged a bullet with that one too. You know what you want. So don't get sucked in by a handsome face and memories, Claire. He hurt you terribly."

It didn't mean he'd hurt her again, though. Necessarily. Eighteen years was a long time. Maybe this was meant to be their second chance. He'd been put in her path. And now he was moving into her rental apartment.

Oh God. Their second chance? Now she was concocting a fantasy about him? Why did he have such a hold on her after all this time?

What she needed to do was to focus on what she wanted out of life: the right partner and a child. That meant really getting out there, and so that was what she would do. She'd kissed her share of frogs since her divorce, but there was bound to be a "prince" out there somewhere. She'd focus on finding him, and then the hold Matt had on her heart, mind and soul would be released.

Right? Yes, right.

"I'll be careful," she promised her sister. "And by the way, I'm open to more blind dates."

"That's my girl," her sister said, stealing a hunk of sesame chicken from her container.

Maybe she'd even join a dating service to speed things up, vet the men via email "chats" before they even met.

"But no matter what, I'm here if you need me," her sister said. Knowingly.

Claire bit her lip. Even her wise sibling knew how strong the Matt Fielding hold was.

Cripes.

"Guess what, Ellie-Belly?" Matt said, sitting down on the round braided rug in his niece's bedroom. *Not bad*, he told himself as he realized he got down on his bad leg in record time and without wincing.

Ellie was playing "dog tea," serving her huge stuffed dogs who were sitting around the rug in a semicircle. Half had fallen over, but she'd prop them back up when it was their time for tea.

"What?" she asked, pouring for the white poodle beside her.

"What do you think about me moving to my own place nearby and fostering Sparkle and training her so that you could adopt her in about a month's time?"

Ellie gasped so loud that his sister came running up the stairs.

"Everything okay?" Laura asked, looking from her daughter to her brother.

Ellie flew into Matt's arms. "Uncle Matt just told me he's going to train Sparkle for me so we can adopt her!"

Laura smiled. "He told me all about it. I'll miss having you around, though, Matt. You just got here."

"I'll be five minutes away," he said. "And, Ellie, you're welcome to come over whenever your mom says it's okay. You can help me train Sparkle."

"This is the best day of my life so far," Ellie said, throwing her arms around Matt for another hug. "Thank you."

"Anything for my favorite niece," Matt said.

"Aren't I your only niece?" Ellie asked.

"What about Sparkle? Isn't she my other niece?"

"I guess she is!" Ellie said. "But don't tell her I'm your favorite. She'll get jealous."

"I won't."

He glanced at Laura, who was smiling. He looked at Ellie, who was also smiling. Even the stuffed dogs were smiling.

But he wondered if Claire was even remotely happy about the situation. She saw a win-win for everyone and had made the offer. But he couldn't imagine she'd be happy having him on her property.

"Matt, could you help me with something downstairs?" his sister asked, gesturing her head toward the door.

He already knew what this was about. When he'd told his sister about Claire's offer, she'd said it sounded like big-time trouble—for Claire. He'd brushed Laura off and finally gotten her okay for Ellie's sake, and then sprinted upstairs to avoid Laura's questions.

Downstairs, she pulled him into the laundry room and shut the door. "Look, it's been almost two decades since you and Claire broke up. So maybe there's no unfinished business. But I'm telling you right now, brother, do not play with that woman's head. Don't start something you can't finish."

"Who says I'm starting anything?"

"Hmm, moving into your first love's house? She's divorced. You're single. Trust me, something is going to happen."

"And?" he asked. Why did he feel so defensive? Because deep down he wanted something to happen? "What if something does?"

"Men." She shook her head slowly. "You're figuring out what to do with your life. Claire Asher is living hers. She's clearly dating. You hurt her once, Matt. All I'm saying is, if you're not sure about her, don't even go there. Leave her be."

"I'm not sure about *anything*," he said.

"Which is why she deserves better than a three-week stand, or however long it takes you to train Sparkle."

He sighed inwardly because his sister was right. As usual.

* * *

The next afternoon, Claire waited for Matt in the gift shop area of the lobby, putting together a box of necessities for Sparkle. She'd included a cute purple collar with white stars, a silver, bone-shaped temporary name tag with Sparkle's name and Matt's cell phone number engraved on it, two different types of leashes, a water bowl, a food bowl, the kibble Sparkle had been eating, a few toys and a packet of information on training and caring for a puppy. Since Matt would be officially fostering the pup, the shelter would take care of Sparkle's vet appointments, and right now the dog was up-to-date on all shots. In about six weeks or so, Sparkle would be ready to be spayed, but right now, all Matt had to focus on was training the pup to live with his sister's family.

When Matt walked in, Claire gave up on pretending she wasn't hopelessly attracted to the man. First love aside, Matt was fostering Sparkle so that his little niece could have the dog she'd fallen in love with. That was pure kindness, especially since Matt had never had a dog nor grown up with one.

"Everything you need for Sparkle is in here," she said quickly, willing herself not to stare at him. "Let's leave this for now, and we'll pick it up when we bring Sparkle through."

"Me, a dog trainer," he said with a smile. "Who knew?"

"What you're doing for your niece is really wonderful," she said as they headed to the kennels.

"I'm just glad I can."

As they entered the kennel area, Matt made a beeline for Hank. "Poor guy," he said. Hank looked at him, staring woefully. The dog got up and walked to the edge of the kennel, and Matt slowly knelt down to say hi. "Hey, guy." Couldn't be so great to be cooped up in there. "Maybe I can take Hank for a walk before we get Sparkle," he said to Claire. "I feel for him."

She smiled. "He'd love it." She picked up a leash from the rack and told Hank to sit, which he did, then she entered the kennel and closed it behind her. She put the leash on, then led him out and latched the kennel again. "There's a path out that side door you can take. It's a quarter-mile loop. I'll go finalize Sparkle's papers, and then we'll be good to go by the time you come back with Hank."

Again, he knelt down beside the senior dog, and she noticed it took him a beat longer than expected. Injury, she figured.

He gave Hank a scratch, then stood up as slowly. "How is this dog still at Furever Paws? He seems like such a good dog—he's calm, he's an old soul and he's awesome looking."

All true, she thought, her heart squeezing for the man and the dog. "I know. But older dogs, especially big ones, tend to languish. We make sure he gets lots of love and TLC."

He nodded and looked at Hank. "See you in a few," he said to Claire.

As she watched him walk away with Hank, she knew she was sunk.

Twenty minutes later, the paperwork was complete and Matt was back, Hank looking quite happy.

"You can do as I did just before," Claire told him, "Lead him in on leash, latch the kennel behind you, unleash him, ask him to sit, then come out and relatch."

"Got it." He did as instructed, standing in front of the kennel as though he was having a hard time walking away.

"And how about a biscuit for being such a great dog?" Claire asked, handing Matt the bone-shaped treat.

Matt slipped it through the kennel bars, and Hank slowly ambled over and picked it up with his mouth, then took it to his bed and began nibbling.

"See you next time, big guy," Matt said.

A few kennels down, Claire had Matt do the same with Sparkle, grabbing her favorite pink-and-purple-striped blankie to put in the box of her things.

"Wow, you are crazy cute," Matt said, kneeling down again and giving Sparkle a pat. "No wonder Ellie went nuts over you."

Sparkle barked up a storm, jumping up on Matt's leg.

"No jump," Claire said firmly. Sparkle remained where she was. "No jump," she repeated, gently moving the dog off Matt. "She'll get the hang of it."

"We'll learn together," he told the puppy. "We're both beginners."

I can help you, she wanted to say. *I'll share everything I know*. But then she'd be with him more than would be healthy for her heart and peace of mind.

In the lobby, Claire grabbed the box of Sparkle's things. She took a final look through, making sure she hadn't forgotten anything.

"What do I owe you for that?" Matt asked, taking out his wallet.

"Oh, since you're fostering, it's on us," she said.

"As a donation then," he said.

That was nice. She named a figure and he walked up to the counter, where Birdie happened to be sitting, training a volunteer on front desk coverage. She could tell Birdie liked Matt's generosity.

"You're doing a wonderful thing by fostering this pup and training her for your niece," Birdie said, giving Matt a serious once-over with her assessing blue eyes. "If you need anything or have any questions, call the shelter anytime. And of course, you'll have one of our best resources steps away," she added, nodding at Claire.

Matt glanced at Claire and smiled, then turned back to Birdie. "Thanks. I appreciate that. And I'm sure I will have many, many questions."

The bell jangled over the front door to Furever Paws, and a thirtyish blonde woman wearing sunglasses and high heels walked in.

"I'd like to adopt a dog," the woman said, despite the fact that Birdie was in midsentence with her trainee. "Small, under twenty pounds. A female. She can't bark. And I don't like dogs with bug eyes." She glanced at Sparkle. "Oh, this one's cute. Did you just adopt her?"

"Yes," Matt said, picking up Sparkle and holding her against his chest, one arm seemingly protecting the puppy from the woman's long pink nails. "She's taken."

Claire stared at the woman. *Bug eyes? I don't like dogs that bark? Exqueeze me?* "Cute indeed but she's a big barker."

The blonde shivered and pushed her big white sunglasses on top of her head. "Oh. Well, I said I wanted a nonbarking dog. I can't stand yippers."

Birdie cleared her throat, her blue eyes steely. "Dogs bark. It's what they do."

Sparkle let out a series of yips to prove Birdie's point.

"My ears," the blonde said, covering them with her hands.

Could she *be* more dramatic?

"We have some beautiful short-haired cats," Claire said to the woman. "Mirabelle is particularly stunning. Cats, of course, don't bark. And they're under twenty pounds."

The woman raised an eyebrow. "Mirabelle? I do like that name. Cats are very queenly. Yes, I'd like to see her."

Birdie smiled and stood. "I'll show you the way."

The woman followed, her heels clicking on the floor.

"Why come in saying you want a dog if you can't handle barking?" Matt asked as they headed for their cars.

"Some folks like the idea of a dog, but the reality is quite different than their fantasy," Claire explained. "And others ignore what they don't want in a pet because they can't resist how the animal looks." She shook her head. "Last week, someone brought back a dog because she didn't like the way it followed her from room to room."

"You're kidding."

She shook her head. "I wish I were. I truly do."

"I guess some people don't know what they're letting themselves in for," Matt said. "Like me."

Claire laughed. "But you're doing this for a good

cause." She reached her car and put the box in the back-seat. "We'll be at the house in no time—Kingdom Creek is just minutes away. I think you'll like the privacy of the development."

"Kingdom Creek. Sounds fancy."

She shrugged. "It was the house I lived in with my husband. Was supposed to be *our* forever home. For a family and two rescue dogs and four cats. Maybe some birds and rabbits too. Now it's just me. And Dempsey, of course. Thank God for Dempsey."

Oh God. Had she said all that? *Our forever home? What was wrong with her? Just stop talking, Claire.*

"How long have you been divorced?" he asked, presumably setting Sparkle down in case she had to do her business. The puppy immediately set to sniffing around her, and Claire focused on that instead of meeting Matt's eyes.

"Three years. He started cheating on me the year prior to our breakup. But he married his affair so he thinks that makes it okay."

She felt her cheeks flush with heat. Hadn't she just told herself to stop talking? The man was making her nervous. That had to be it.

"Cheating is never okay," Matt said, holding her gaze for a second. "I'm sorry you went through all that."

"What's that saying? What doesn't kill you makes you stronger?" *I got through you, Matt Fielding—of course I got through my divorce.*

"Don't I know it," he said with a kind of wistful nod.

"Guess we've both been through a thing or two."

He nodded again. "We both had been through a thing or two when we were a couple, Claire. I'd lost my brother. You'd lost your dad. It's always friggen something."

"Yeah," she said. "It is. Thank God for cuddly dogs, huh?"

He smiled and scooped Sparkle up, giving her a nuzzle. "I'll be right behind you." He nodded at the car next to hers.

A lone duffel was in the backseat. Was that everything he had? She supposed he couldn't accumulate a life's worth of possessions while on multiple tours of duty.

Fifteen minutes. And then Matt Fielding would be moving into her house, their bedrooms separated only by drywall. It had to be the worst—and best—idea she ever had.

"And this is the bedroom," Claire said as Matt followed her into the large room of the second-floor apartment.

He liked the place. The apartment was a decent size, the living room spacious, with French doors leading to the small deck and stairs down to the backyard. That was his entrance, so he wouldn't necessarily run into Claire unless she happened to be out with Dempsey in this part of the yard. The bathroom had a big tub and spa-type shower, which was a plus when you were six foot one. He barely noticed the kitchen since he didn't cook much, other than basic spaghetti with jarred marinara sauce and never-toasted-right toast. But he did notice the windows—lots of them. Matt could breathe here, relax here. Considering that the proximity of Claire Asher made those things difficult from the get-go, it was a real testament to how comfortable he felt in the apartment.

He put his duffel bag on the queen-size bed. He and Claire had created a lot of memories in their two years as a teenage couple, but "the bedroom" hadn't been a part of them. He'd barely touched her, though he'd been dying to. Hands skimming over her shirts and sweaters, sometimes slipping underneath. That was as far as they'd gone in those days. They'd been lip-locked constantly, and he'd fantasized every night about sex and particularly sex with Claire Asher. Now, standing inches from a bed, her light perfume enveloping him, awareness of her driving him mad, he wanted to lie down and take her with him.

Instead, he leaned down to give Sparkle a pat for being a good dog and not barking or peeing on the rug, as she'd done on the tour of the kitchen. Claire hadn't blinked. She'd grabbed paper towels, followed up with a Swiffer and that had been that. "It's a nice place. Don't you agree, Sparkle? A good training center for you."

Sparkle barked twice, looking up at him. The bedroom carpet was soft, which had to be a plus for a little dog.

"I'll take that as a yes," Claire said with a smile. "Okay, back to the kitchen. I have a whole folder of info for you."

"Info?" he repeated, following her down the hall.

"For your new life as a foster dad who'll be training a five-month-old puppy."

As she turned to head out of the bedroom, he reached for her hand, and she whirled around.

"I'm not even sure if I said thank you. For this," he

added, gesturing at the room. "You saved the day for my family. Now I have an excited niece, a not-pissed-off sister and a not-pissed-off brother-in-law."

She laughed. "Well, the apartment was empty and the situation presented itself, so..."

"So, here we are."

"Here we are," she repeated, then cleared her throat and turned to go again. This *had* to be kind of uncomfortable for her. It sure as hell was for him. But in equally good and bad ways.

Back in the small white kitchen, Claire picked up a folder and opened it. "Okay, straight to business. This contains everything you need to know about training lessons and basic puppy care."

The little brown-and-white dog began turning in circles, trying to catch her tail, which was her trademark move. "Hey, Sparkle," Matt said.

The dog ignored him.

"Sparkle," Matt said again.

Ignored by a twelve-pound spinning pooch.

"Page two," Claire said, pointing at the folder. She turned to the bags she'd brought from the shelter, and took out a pack of small training treats.

She held a treat in her hand, her fist closed over it, and waved it near the dog. "Sparkle."

The dog stopped and looked at her hand.

"Yup, she definitely smells the treat. She can't see it, but she can smell it." The dog sniffed around. "Sparkle!" Claire said again.

The dog looked at her.

"Good dog!" Claire said, and gave her the treat. "We're teaching Sparkle her name. Every time you say her name and she looks at you—actually makes eye contact—give her a tiny treat. After she associates the word Sparkle with a treat, she'll realize she gets a treat every time she acknowledges it. Then we'll move on to calling her from another room."

"Huh. I guess I always wondered how dogs learned their names."

"I do expect you to do your homework," she said, pointing at the folder.

"Yes, Teacher. I absolutely will."

She smiled, and it lit up her entire face. "Now for a housetraining lesson. The plan will be to take Sparkle out first thing in the morning, then every hour, immediately after she eats, after she wakes from a nap and before bed. She'll get used to the idea that doing her business is meant for outside, not inside."

"Did you say every hour?"

Claire laughed. "It'll take a few days, but then you can stop that and move to after meals and naps."

"Well, Sparkle," he said, and before he could continue, the little spinning creature looked right at him! "Hey, she looked at me!" He reached into the bag for a treat and gave it to her. Sparkle sure did like these treats.

"Perfect. It really happens fast. In a couple of days, she'll know it's her name, and we can work on more commands like *come* and *stay*."

"You're a good dog," he said to Sparkle. The puppy turned and looked at him, which earned her another treat.

Claire smiled. "So she's had a few treats, and she last went potty on the kitchen floor. We don't want her to associate eliminating with the kitchen, so let's take her out. If she pees or poops, she gets a treat."

"Will she gain a hundred pounds?" he asked.

Claire smiled. "These treats are tiny and temporary. Plus, Sparkle is so busy and will get so much exercise running around the fenced yard that she can have all the treats she deserves."

"Key word is deserves, I figure," he said.

"Absolutely. No treats for just being adorable."

He laughed. "I'm getting the hang of this."

She handed him the leash. "Let's take her outside."

He followed her through the French doors to the small deck, and then down the stairs to the fenced yard.

Sparkle did her business, which got her a "good dog" and a treat. This dog training business was going all right so far.

"Well, I have two classes of essays to grade," she said. "But text or call if you need me."

Wait. You're leaving? Suddenly Matt felt a little out of his element at the idea of being all alone with the puppy. Sparkle was sturdy enough, he supposed, but there was something fragile about her too. She was a baby. Maybe that was it. "What should I do with her?" he asked.

Claire laughed. "Well, you could play with her out here, just watch her explore the yard and sniff around. Then you can take her upstairs and let her get acclimated to the apartment, show her where her crate and bed are, her food bowls, that kind of thing."

"And then what?"

She tilted her head, looking at him as if he'd gone a little crazy. "And then you just be."

"Be?"

"You go about your life. Unpack. Make yourself a cup of coffee. Take a shower. Watch TV. She'll do her thing. You'll be sitting on the couch and might find her trying to jump up to curl up next to you."

"Is she allowed on the couch?" he asked.

"This is a very dog-centric house," she said. "So, yes."

Sparkle came back over and sniffed his shoe, then looked up at him expectantly. He had a feeling she wanted another treat.

"I guess I'll let her explore out here a bit more, and then take her up. I can do my homework while she explores her new digs. I have to read up on the crate training thing."

"Well, I'm here if you need me," she said, kneeling down to pet Sparkle. Then she stood back up and entered the house through the sliding glass door beyond her patio. Right under his deck.

The minute she was gone, he missed her.

"It's just you and me, Sparkle," he said. He threw one of the little balls he'd stuffed in his other pocket—the one that wasn't chock-full of treats—and Sparkle went flying after it. He laughed. "Fetch!" he called. She did not fetch. In fact, she ignored the ball in favor of a leaf being tossed around in the breeze. He laughed and watched the pup explore the yard, sniffing at every blade of grass, and, ten minutes later, he realized he felt something he hadn't in a long time.

Almost relaxed.

Chapter Five

The force of the explosion propelled him backward and he slammed against a tree, his leg twisted at a strange angle, warm, sticky blood running down his temple. McCubbers. He had to check on McCubbers... He could hear whimpering. Fear. Pain. The sound— that whimpering—was inside his head, all around him. McCubbers, I'm trying to get to you...

Matt bolted upright, his breath ragged. Again, the soft bedding confused him until he realized he wasn't in Afghanistan; he was in his new apartment at Claire's house. He took in the pale gray walls, slightly illuminated by the moon, and the dresser with the square mirror over it. He closed his eyes and took a deep, calming breath.

Damn nightmare. Always the same one.

Except he could still hear the whimpering.

McCubbers definitely never made a high-pitched sound like that. Where the hell was it coming from? He glanced around for the source of the sound.

His gaze landed on the kennel across from his bed. Sparkle stood by the door, whining and whimpering.

"Hey, there," he said, getting out of bed. "Someone has to go outside?" He glanced at the time on his phone. Only 3:13 a.m. Such was the life of a puppy trainer. He slid his feet into his sneakers, put on his leather jacket, then unlatched the kennel and took Sparkle outside and down the deck stairs, trying to be quiet so as not to wake Claire. He had no idea where her bedroom was in relation to his deck or this part of the yard.

He led Sparkle to the grass on the far side of the yard. "Go potty," he whispered to the pup, per what he'd read in the pile of training articles Claire had given him. Apparently, it was a good idea for a dog to have a "spot," so they'd do their business quickly—a good thing in the middle of the night and when it was freezing. Right now, it was both. He still had two treats in his pocket, and gave one to Sparkle with a "good dog."

Back upstairs, he took off his jacket and sneakers, gave the little dog a pat, then put her back in the kennel and got into bed. Man, these sheets were soft. And the down comforter and pillows were already lulling him to sleep.

Whimper. Whine. Whiiiine. Whimper.

He peeled open an eye. "How am I supposed to sleep with that racket?" he asked Sparkle.

More whimpering. More whining.

"I'm not supposed to reward that," he said, getting out of bed again. "Tell you what. If you stop making those annoying sounds, I'll let you out for a little while. You can understand a bargain, right, Sparkle?"

And don't tell my sister, he added silently as he walked to the kennel. Sparkle immediately piped down. She looked positively thrilled when Matt opened the door. He scooped her up and brought up to his bed, the little brown-and-white mutt curling up beside him. She leaned over and licked his arm, then got up, turned around in a circle three times and settled back down with a sigh.

Dogs sighed? Who knew?

Her little eyes closed.

"Hey, wait a minute, sneaky. You can't get comfortable. You have to sleep in your kennel."

Sparkle started snoring, another thing he didn't know dogs did. The sturdy little weight of her felt kind of comforting next to him, and honestly, Matt was too tired to put her back in the kennel. He'd confess to Claire in the morning and see how bad an infraction it was.

"I'm already in the doghouse with Claire just by virtue of being me," he whispered to Sparkle, who opened her eyes as if she really was listening. "So best behavior tomorrow, got it?"

Sparkle got up and came closer, licked his face and burrowed her way under the comforter, stretching out on her side against his rib cage. He smiled and shook his head, giving her exposed belly a gentle rub.

"Who's training who here?" he whispered as the dog's eyes closed.

* * *

As Claire was bringing Dempsey outside the next morning at 6:00 a.m., she saw Matt in the yard, tossing a ball for Sparkle. The puppy did not fetch. She tilted her head and went running in the opposite direction.

Claire laughed and reached into her pockets for her fleece gloves. It was pretty chilly this morning. "Well, we can work on fetch once she's got the basics down."

Matt whirled around as though surprised to see her. "I thought fetch was hardwired into dogs," he said with that killer smile.

How could he look this good at six in the morning, with hardly any sleep? At around 3:00 a.m., she'd heard him open the door to his deck and go outside. She'd forced herself to stay in bed and not tiptoe over to watch him. Of course, she'd lain awake for more than an hour, remembering, wondering, thinking. She must have kissed Matt Fielding three thousand times in the two years they'd been a couple. Being in his arms or holding his hand or having his arm slung around her shoulders had always felt so good, so comforting, so right.

He'd told her that he was a virgin too and that he wanted his first time to be with her, but he wouldn't pressure her—he wanted her to tell him when she was ready. She'd felt ready but afraid in a way she couldn't explain to herself, let alone him, so she'd started telling him she'd be ready on prom night. Far enough away that she could mentally and emotionally prepare herself. For what, she didn't know. Sex, particularly with the love of her life, had seemed huge, monumental— the biggest deal in the world.

And then instead of sneaking off to a motel at midnight after the prom in their high school gym, where she and Matt had slow danced and kissed through most of the songs, he'd broken up with her. In his car, in the high school parking lot. He'd said he was sorry, but it had to be over between them, it was for the best; she'd see. She'd been so speechless she couldn't even form words in her head beyond *What?* And then she'd gone running from his car, her high-heeled sandals in her hand, and because she lived three houses from the school, he'd let her go.

All that next day she'd forced herself not to call him, storm his house, demand to know what the hell he was doing to them. She'd lasted two hours. She'd pounded on the Fieldings' door, but his mother had told Claire that Matt wasn't home, that he'd started his own pre-boot-camp regimen and was probably at the high school field. She'd wanted to rush over there but hadn't, hoping, praying he'd come for her once some time, meaning hours, had passed. He hadn't. So she'd gone to his house again, his mother casting compassionate glances at her as Matt reiterated everything he'd said the night before. It was for the best, he was leaving in the morning, separate paths, separate ways. He'd been so resolute, no tears in his eyes, when Claire had been gushing tears and choking on her sobs to the point that his mother had come into the kitchen with tissues and then hurried out to give them privacy again.

That was the last time she'd seen Matt Fielding until the other day at Furever Paws.

Her sister had said it was a good thing she hadn't lost

her virginity to Matt, but Claire had always wished she had. That way, she could have hated him for using her for sex, *then* dumping her. Instead, he'd kept his hands to himself. Ugh, the whole thing was so complicated. Good guy one way. Jerk another.

But still so freaking gorgeous. And sexy. All that sunlit thick, brown hair. The intense blue eyes framed by long, dark lashes. His shoulders in that black leather jacket. His long, muscular legs in those worn jeans. Matt was pure hotness. Always had been, but now the tall, lanky guy he'd been had been replaced with a man.

Stop staring, she ordered herself.

Oh gosh—what had he said? Something about fetch being hardwired into dogs. "Well, the springer spaniel side of Sparkle has the retrieving thing to a science, but whatever she's mixed with might not."

"Ah, makes sense. I still have a lot to learn," he said. "How bad is it that I let Sparkle sleep on my bed last night?"

He'd always been a softie. Except when it came to not dumping her, that was. "It can be irresistible to let a dog—especially a puppy—sleep with you. It's really up to you, well, your sister and what her future plans are. If she's going to let Sparkle sleep with Ellie, then it's fine. Otherwise, it's better to get her used to sleeping in the kennel for consistency."

"Got it. I'll have to ask Laura. She can be a real marshmallow about some things. I can see her letting Sparkle sleep with Ellie. I know that's what Ellie will want, for sure."

Claire was about to respond when raised voices coming from the house next door stopped her.

"I'm not breaking up with her, and you can't make me!" a boy's voice hiss-whispered from the next yard.

"She's all wrong for you!" a woman's voice said. "She's trouble and she'll bring you down. Suddenly you're thinking of *not* going to college? Over my dead body!"

"Whatever!" the boy shouted. Then a door slammed.

Claire glanced at Matt and whispered, "Seventeen-year-old Justin next door. For the past few months I've never seen him without a long-haired blonde."

"Blondes are trouble for sure," he said, reaching out to move a strand of hair the wind had blown across her cheek.

Claire froze, his touch so unexpected and so undeniably welcome that she couldn't speak.

"Sorry. Overstepped," he said, moving backward a bit. "I—" He clamped down on whatever he'd been about to say.

"If anyone's trouble, it's first loves living on your property, making you remember the good ole days." *Oh God.* Had she really just said that? *Sure, Claire, open up that can o' worms. Are you crazy?*

"Tell me about it," he said. "I was up half the night remembering."

"What were you remembering?" she asked. Because she couldn't resist. And she had to know.

"How crazy about you I was," he said.

"I thought you were. In fact, I thought you were as

crazy about me as I was for you. But you dumped me. Remember that?"

Oh God, again. Had she actually said *that*? What was the point of having this discussion almost two decades later? *Lame, Claire.*

But then again, they'd never had this discussion. He'd broken her heart and then he was gone. Until a few days ago. So why not have it out, right here, right now? Being around Matt made her feel like that seventeen-year-old girl—in love, the whole world in front of her, everything possible. Until it wasn't.

He turned away, his attention on Sparkle for a moment as the little dog sniffed a tree trunk a few feet away. "I 'dumped' you because I was trouble."

"Oh, right. The imminent soldier, about to go off to serve his country, enlisting in his fallen brother's memory. Oh yeah, you were big trouble."

"I mean that I would have held you back," he said, his gaze on her. "You wanted so much back then. You had so many dreams and plans. And I didn't have any of that in me."

"Funny how I managed to be so in love with you," she said, shaking her head.

"I honestly don't know why you were. I had nothing to offer to you. I have less to offer you now. If I wanted to, I mean. If you wanted to—Oh, earth, swallow me up," he said, shaking his head. "Forget everything I just said. I'm just saying I would have held you back."

"Why would you make that decision for me?" she asked.

"Because I loved you that much, Claire. That's why."

He looked at her, then at the ground, as if coming to some kind of decision. "I have some calls to make. Sparkle, come on, girl."

The dog glanced at him. He pulled a treat from the pocket of his leather jacket and the dog came running over. "Good, Sparkle," he said, holding out his palm. She grabbed the treat and followed him as he started for the stairs.

Because I loved you that much… Claire was so choked up she couldn't speak. And what would she say anyway? All of that was so far in the past.

I have even less to offer you now.

If that was how he felt, then he surely wasn't going to be her husband and the father of her children.

Do. Not. Get. Sucked. Into. The. Past. This man just told you he's not going to be what you want or need. Believe him. Don't be a fool.

But people could change their minds. People's minds could be changed.

Now she was arguing with herself?

There was only one way to nip this in the ole bud— take charge of herself before Matt Fielding got under her skin.

"Hey, Matt," she called up to where he was on the deck landing.

He stopped and looked down at her—clearly bracing himself for what she was going to say. Because regardless of how much time had passed between then and now, she knew him. For a moment, she let herself take him in, the way the morning sunlight hit his hair.

"You're doing great with Sparkle," she said.

She could actually see his shoulders relax.

"Thanks," he said. "My teacher prepared some great material, and I read the homework assignments."

She smiled up at him and nodded. He went inside, closing the sliding glass door behind him.

Yup, that's right, Asher. Keep it focused on the dog. Lighthearted. All about the dog. Because you're getting Matt Fielding out of your system right now. That was the only way she'd survive sharing her home, her yard, her love of dogs with him. She had to create barriers and distance.

She had to find the man she was looking for. The man she'd share her life with. A husband. A father for the child she wanted. Matthew Fielding was not that man.

She went back inside and fired up her laptop, typing *dating sites* into the search engine. There were so many, some easy to nix because of their ridiculous names, like Hotties4U.com. Her gaze stopped on SecondChance-Sweethearts.com. Now that was more Claire's style. And this was all about a second chance at love, right?

She clicked onto the Create A Profile page. Hmm, she needed a user name. She typed in *AlwaysLearning*. "What are the three qualities that best describe you in a nutshell?" How was she supposed to answer that? She grabbed her phone and texted her sister with the question.

Della responded right away. Are you taking a Cosmo quiz or filling out a dating profile? Hoping for the latter!

Latter. Help!

Kind. Responsible. Seeking. Sounds a little dry but hey, you want to weed out the sex fiends and idiots.

That's definitely true. Seeking? Seeking what?

That's for him to find out. Many hims!

Ah. Her sister was good at these things.

She wrote her paragraph about her interests, blah, blah, blah, how much she loved teaching, about helping young people light up about books and express themselves, that she loved old movies and superhero flicks, that she could eat pasta every night for the rest of her life and never get bored, that she was looking for a man who was ready to start a family. She deleted that last part, then re-added it. That *was* what she was looking for. A life partner. A husband. A father for her children. So it made no sense *not* to put it out there.

She uploaded a recent photo, one Della had taken at her husband's birthday dinner party two months ago. Not too close up, not too far away, head to toe.

She paid up her $14.95 for a one-month membership and hit Submit before she could chicken out.

Take that, Matt Fielding.

Not five minutes later, as Claire was about to check her SecondChanceSweethearts account to see if she had any messages from hordes of men "wanting to know her better," the doorbell rang. Dempsey shot up with a bark and hurried to the door, staring at it.

She finished filling up her mug with toffee-flavored coffee and set it down, then walked over to the door. "Hey, Dempsey, maybe the perfect man is at the door, sent by SecondChanceSweehearts." Now, granted, she always talked to Dempsey regardless of the boxer mix's ability to respond. But she still might be losing her mind if she expected her Mr. Right to be at the door.

Actually, it was Matt Fielding at the door.

"I thought I should formally ring the doorbell rather than just go down the deck steps to your side door," he explained.

The side door was completely private, opening to the fenced-in yard, with evergreens completely blocking the view to the next house. She rarely closed the curtains since no one could see her sitting in her living room, watching a romantic comedy with Dempsey and a big bowl of popcorn. But now, anytime Matt came down those steps, he would see her.

"Everything okay?" she asked.

He nodded, then gave Dempsey, who stood beside her, a scratch on the head. "Just thought you should know the stair railing on the left side heading upstairs is loose. I could easily take care of it. I'm a trained mechanic, so I'm generally pretty handy if anything needs to be fixed. You refused to take any rent while I'm living here, so I insist on offering my services in trade."

She thought of Matt in her living room, kitchen, bedroom…a tool belt slung low on his hips, fixing all manner of things as she watched his muscles ripple and his very sexy rear fill out the faded old jeans he wore. "A cabinet in the kitchen has a loose hinge, and I never get around to finding the power drill," she said. "And I've been wanting to bolt the bookcase in the living room to the wall. You're going to be sorry you asked. I can probably come up with a list of ten things I've been meaning to call someone about."

Wait a minute, dummy! Was she really finding stuff for Matt to do inside her home? What the heck was wrong with her?

You want to be around him. And not just to stare at him when you think he doesn't notice.

"I can take care of all that," he said. "I assume you're working today—I can come back at three thirty if that's good for you."

Tell him it's not. Tell him you'll fix all the stuff yourself, or that you forgot you already hired a handyman. Tell him anything, but don't let him inside your home! "That works," she heard herself say. "I'm not due at Furever Paws till five today to help close up for the night."

"See you then," he said with a nod to Dempsey, and then disappeared down the stairs.

Fool, she chastised herself as she closed the door. *Your knees can barely hold you up when you look at Matt. Now, he's going to be in your kitchen and living room on a regular basis.*

She had no doubt she'd find some reason to get him in her bedroom. That was how ridiculously attracted to him she was. Had it just been too long since she'd been with a man? Did *since her divorce* count as too long?

Way too long, her sister had said, which was why she'd begun setting Claire up with anyone who was single.

Ding!

Claire went to her laptop on the desk in the living

room. She had four messages from the dating website. *That was fast.*

And necessary. Because if Matt was going to be Mr. Fix It in her home, she'd need more than a distraction from him. She'd need to know she was taking steps to protect herself from getting wrapped up in the past, in hoping for something that couldn't be.

HOT4U, whose profile photos were all shirtless, loved "quiet nights at home with his special lady." *Yeah, no doubt. Next!* Except the next two weren't much better. Online dating might not be the way to go. Hadn't her friend and fellow teacher Sandy mentioned that she had a single cousin who might be "just right for you"? She should forget online dating and focus on fix-ups from trustworthy people.

Claire took a fast look at the fourth message. Hmm. BigReader had one photo, a side view of an attractive, dark-haired man on a boat of some kind. He was thirty-seven, an accountant, loved historical biographies, and here was the big one: he loved dogs.

Claire hit reply.

Within twenty minutes, she had a date for dinner tomorrow night.

Matt spent the day working with Sparkle and showing the little pup around town. He'd run into some old friends and now had plans for barbecue—"feel free to bring a date"—and beers at the dive bar on the outskirts of town.

"Didn't take you for the kind of guy who'd have some fluffy puppy with a purple collar," his old rival on the baseball team had said. Before he could say a word, a buddy had added, "Matt has a thigh-to-shin gash in his leg from his service to our country, so shut up." The rival had stuck his hand out and Matt shook it, and just like that, he was one of the guys again. But did he really want to make friends, build any kind of life here when he'd run into Claire all the time? No. He'd train the puppy for Ellie, fix all the broken things in Claire's house and then ride into the unknown. At least that was a plan, even if there was no actual plan.

He'd have to leave town. He'd thought about Claire all day—from old memories to how she'd looked this morning. Claire owned a house. She had an important career. She was passionate about her volunteer work. She had everything. And Matt? At this point, all he had was a duffel bag of clothes and a twelve-pound puppy that he'd be handing over once she was trained. *So leave your fantasies about her in your head*, he reminded himself as, tool belt on and power drill in hand, he rang her doorbell at three thirty. *Don't think about kissing her, even though you want to. Don't imagine her naked, even though you can't help it. Don't picture the two of you in bed, despite being unable to shake the image.*

She opened the door, and he immediately thought about kissing her—dropping the power drill on the floor and telling her he'd been able to think of little else but her since he'd run into her at the shelter his first full day home. But Dempsey was standing guard next to her, as always, peering up at him with those soulful eyes, reminding him of his promise to himself—and secretly, to her. Not to get involved. Claire Asher had always deserved better than him, better than what he could offer.

She wore a blue velvet jacket and a black-and-white skirt. Her teacher clothes. She smelled fantastic, like spicy flowers. Her hair was in a low bun and man, did he want to feel those silky blond tresses running through his fingers.

"I just got home," she said, opening the door wider and gesturing for him to enter. "I'll go change and meet you back in the living room. You can check out the bookcase that I want anchored. I keep being afraid that a dog Dempsey's size could pull it down if she jumped up. Hasn't happened yet, but it worries me."

"I'll take care of it," he said. He went to kneel down, and for some reason today—maybe the threat of rain in the air—he winced and it took double the usual time to get down. But he was halfway there and it would hurt worse to stand back up, so he balanced himself on the edge of the couch and eased into the kneel. *Don't say anything. Don't ask*, he sent telepathically to Claire as she gave Dempsey a rigorous pat on her soft but bristly fur. Sparkle was like a down pillow compared to Dempsey.

"War injury?" she asked.

Crud. He hated when attention was called to it, even though the ole bad leg had given him a pass for carting around such a too-cute puppy in a striped purple collar this morning.

He nodded, focusing on Dempsey. "IED."

Now it was her turn to wince. "Does it hurt much?"

Crud again. He didn't want that look in her eyes.

Concern. Worry. Claire was a runner, or at least she had been, and back when they were a couple she was even faster than him. Now, he wasn't even sure he could walk a half mile, let alone run a 5K.

"Sometimes," he admitted.

"Sorry," she said.

He pulled himself up, wincing again, and he saw her reach her arm out as if to steady him if he needed it. This was exactly what he wanted to avoid. Feeling like half a man. He mentally shook his head away from those "poor me" bullcrap thoughts; he was lucky as hell and he knew it. Two in his unit had come back with much worse injuries.

"I'll go check out the bookcase," he said, heading over to it without looking at her.

He could feel her lingering in the room, and knew she was wondering if she should say something, do something. How could he know her so well after all this time? Maybe when it came to the important people in your life, those who got under your skin, those who helped make you who you were, that feeling of "knowing them" never went away.

Great.

The bookcase. *Focus on the damned bookcase*, he told himself. He heard the soft click of Dempsey's nails on the hardwood floor, which meant Claire was leaving the room and Dempsey was following. *Good.*

The bookcase was waist-high and full of interesting things, like the stained-glass jewelry box he knew she'd inherited from her great-grandmother when she was sixteen, a lopsided vase she'd made in pottery class back in high school, a lot of books and family photos. On the top of the bookshelf was an open photo album. *Whoa.* The page was full of photos of him and Claire as a couple and some of him solo. He put down the power drill and picked up the album.

Had he really ever been that young? From seventeen to a hundred.

He turned to the first page and looked at each photo, smiling at Claire as a toddler with birthday cake all over her face, Claire as a little girl on a two-wheeler, her beloved father holding on to the back of the seat, Claire as a sixteen-year-old, with a tall, skinny boy standing a respectful distance away for the photo. *God, look at me,* he thought, *madly in love, afraid to show it, barely able to believe she liked me back.*

"Oh, um, I—" Claire said.

He turned around, still holding the album. Claire's cheeks were red, as though she were embarrassed at having been caught reminiscing. Which was exactly what he was doing now. She'd changed into jeans and a yellow sweater, and reminded him of the girl he'd known, who used to drive him wild just by existing.

"I can't believe I was ever that young," he said, his gaze back on the photograph of the two of them. "Or that the most beautiful girl in the world was mine." Okay, that had come out of his mouth without his say-so. But he sure had been thinking it. Back then and now. He stared down at the book and flipped the page. He and Claire dancing at prom. Kissing.

She walked over to him and glanced at the page. She pointed at the top left photo, of the two of them arm in arm for the "professional" couple shot the principal had taken of all the attendees. "I sure had no idea then what was going to happen by the end of the night. I thought my boyfriend and I would be sneaking off to a motel. Instead, I was sobbing in my room with a pillow over my head."

Punch to the gut. He hated how much he'd hurt her back then. "If you had any idea how much I wanted you that night, Claire," he said, putting the album down. He took her hands, and she looked up at him. "I was madly in love with you."

"I don't want to talk about the past," she said. "What I want is for you to kiss me."

Me too, he thought, everything else fading away. Like reason and the real world. He stepped closer and put his hands on her beautiful face, then leaned in to kiss her, gently and sweetly in case she changed her mind midway.

But that didn't seem to happen because she deepened the kiss, snaking her hands through his hair. She kiss-walked him backward to the couch and straddled him, trailing kisses along his neck. He was going to explode.

And then she began unbuttoning his shirt, her hands cool on his hot skin. Five seconds later, he had her sweater off, one hand slipping down under the waistband of her soft, sexy jeans.

"Help me get you out of my system," she whispered in his ear. "This is what I need."

He pulled back, her words a splash of cold water on his head. "What?"

"You and me," she said. "It's not going to happen—in

the long run, right? Just like last time. So let me get you out of my system once and for all." She ran her hands inside his shirt, over his chest.

It felt so good. But he didn't believe her. So he pulled away and stood up.

"You think sex will get me out of your system?" He shook his head. "I already think about you all damned day, Claire. Sex will make me unable to do anything else. Sparkle will be peeing all over the apartment."

"So once again you're not going to sleep with me for my own good?" She walked away and stopped by the sliding glass door, then turned to glare at him. "How about you let me make my own decisions for *myself.*"

"I won't sleep with you when I know I'm leaving soon," he said. "If that's 'like last time,' then so be it. I'm wrong for you. Just like eighteen years ago."

"I think I hear Sparkle whimpering," she said through gritted teeth, crossing her arms over her chest.

"No, you don't," he said. He'd become attuned to every little noise the puppy made over the past couple of days. If Sparkle had made a single peep, he'd have heard it. Claire wanted him gone, but shouldn't they talk about this? Shouldn't they get it straight and right between them? She had to understand where he was coming from.

She lifted her chin. "I have to grade essays. So this isn't a good day for you to work in the house, after all."

This wasn't what he wanted either. This bad kind of tension between them. He hated the thought of leaving this way.

"Claire, if you only knew—"

She held up a hand. "Matt, you've said it all. You find me attractive, but can't—on all levels. Have I got that right?"

Oh hell.

Her phone rang and so he headed to the door. *Don't say you're sorry or she'll conk you over the head*, he told himself.

So, he didn't, but he wanted to. He *was* sorry. And wished things could be different. Wished *he* were different.

Chapter Six

Ridiculous. This morning, Claire had been sure the way to get Matt Fielding out of her system was to spend $14.95 on an online dating service. Suddenly, just several hours later, the way to get over him was to ravish his body in her bed? To finally have sex with him? Was she insane?

Thank God he'd put the kibosh on that. Right? She went back and forth, depending on the minute. Yes, it was a good thing. She'd be a mess if she finally slept with the man she couldn't get over after eighteen years. And she couldn't afford to be an emotional mess. She had hormonal, pimply faced, identity-seeking preteens depending on her to be the calm, rational one. She had a foster dog who needed to be fed, exercised and played with. And she needed to be present for the dogs at Furever Paws, not be all teary-eyed and unfocused.

So, yes, score one for Matt. But then she'd think that maybe sex with him really would do the job, that the mystery of him, of "it," would *poof!*—disappear. She'd know what sex with him was like, and she'd move on. Wasn't that a possibility?

Luckily, Claire really didn't have time to vacillate endlessly about sleeping with Matt or not. She was due at Furever Paws at five, and then she was meeting Big-Reader, aka Connor Hearon, at the Main Street Grille at seven for dinner. He'd said during their two message exchanges that it was unusual to make dinner plans before spending much time emailing back and forth and chatting on the phone, but he had "a feeling about her." Claire, unfortunately, had lost all feeling and interest in meeting Connor, but she was not going to let Matt derail another date with a potential beau who could be what she needed and wanted right now. To be safe, she'd texted her friend and fellow Furever Paws volunteer, Amanda Sylvester, manager and co-owner of the Main Street Grille, to let her know she was meeting an online date there at seven and to keep an eye out for anything strange. Not that Claire knew what that would constitute. It just seemed a good precaution. Then she texted her sister BigReader's details as a "just in case" too.

You're my hero, her sister texted. Very happy you're putting yourself out there. This time next year, rock-a-bye baby... :)

Getting a little ahead of yourself, there, sister dear,

Claire thought. But at least Della had made her smile. Because was putting herself out there supposed to feel this…unexciting? Once again, she blamed Matt Fielding.

That really was handy, sticking him with the blame for everything.

Matt wanted to pick up another pack of training treats for Sparkle, so he drove out to Furever Paws. He could probably find the same treats at the supermarket, but he liked the idea of spending his money at the shelter. And he'd run out of places to go to avoid going home—he still felt funny thinking of the apartment at Claire's as home, but it was for now. Since their argument, he'd vacuumed all the dog hair and errant treats around the apartment, gone grocery shopping, returned his "not him" rental car and bought himself a used black Mustang from a car dealer he'd heard good things about. Then he'd spent a couple of hours in the park with Sparkle and worn the puppy out. They'd practiced commands—*come* and *stay*—and Sparkle was getting the hang of it. A woman had come over, oohing and aahing over Sparkle's cuteness, and because it was such a small world, she turned out to be his niece Ellie's third-grade teacher. Mrs. Panetta, whom he'd heard Ellie rave about, gave Sparkle an A+ for cuteness and her *stay* command.

When he'd left the pup at home ten minutes ago, she was fast asleep in the kennel, curled up with her bounty of toys in her little bed.

Matt pulled into a spot in the small gravel parking lot

at Furever Paws. Huge oak trees surrounded the sturdy, dark-gray, one-story building. He walked up the porch steps, the logo—a large image of a cat and dog silhouetted inside a heart—painted on the front greeting him. He pulled open the glass door and walked into the small lobby. He remembered tall, gray-haired Birdie, one of the owners, from the last time he was here.

"Afternoon, ma'am," he said. "I'm Ma—"

Birdie turned her sharp blue eyes from the computer screen to him. "You left here a few days ago with one of our not-ready-for-prime-time pups," she said, her stern expression softening into a smile. "I know exactly who you are. It's nice to see you again, Matt. And call me Birdie. I'm not the ma'am type. *Pleeeze.*"

He laughed. "Well, Birdie, I'm here to pick up some more training treats for Sparkle. We're going to work on the *lie down* command tomorrow."

"Our gift shop has plenty," she said, gesturing to the wall along the side of the lobby. Claire had mentioned that the supplies were mostly donated; sales benefited the shelter, and he was glad to help.

He heard barking coming from down a long hallway behind the lobby. He could see a couple of doors marked Staff Only, and one at the far end that said Veterinary Clinic. There were two additional rooms, one marked Cats and one marked Dogs. From his vantage point, he could see through the large glass window of the Dogs room; a couple was sitting down and petting Tucker, the little chiweenie who seemed a lot more interested in them than he'd been in Matt and Ellie the other day.

The woman in the room tried to pick up Tucker and

got barked at; Matt could hear the loud barks from where he stood. Then another woman moved into view—and Matt would know that blond hair anywhere. Claire. How had he forgotten that she'd said she'd be volunteering at five? "He will not do at all!" the woman snapped as she opened the door and huffed out, followed by her husband and an exasperated Claire, with little Tucker on a leash.

Maybe he's nervous and doesn't want to be picked up by a total stranger who's hovering over him, he wanted to shout. *Jeez.*

"Perhaps you could come to our adoption event his weekend," Claire was saying. "Many of our adoptable dogs are with foster parents, but they'll all be here this Saturday and Sunday."

"Well, if they're less ferocious than him," the man said.

Matt almost burst out laughing. Tucker was what—thirteen pounds soaking wet?

"Tucker isn't ferocious," Claire said, and Matt was impressed by the warmth in her voice. "Just a combination of timid and stressed."

"Well, you did tell us he could be skittish and barky," the woman said, her tone calmer. "My fault for insisting on meeting him just because he sounded cute."

Huh. Now Matt could see why Claire's way—being civil and kind and gently explaining—was smarter than his, which would have been to tell the woman she didn't seem like a dog person.

And he was starting to become one himself. So he sort of knew.

"Tucker could use a dedicated foster parent, but right now, all our foster homes are full," Claire added.

The woman eyed Tucker with disdain. Humph.

"He's not the one," the man with her said. "We're looking for 'just right.' A dog with a certain personality."

Matt sighed. From everything he'd read, even the most "just right" rescue dog wouldn't show his true personality till he or she was settled and comfortable in a new home. Basic temperament, sure. But personality would take time to emerge.

"Well, we'll be back Saturday," the woman said, and the couple headed for the door.

He watched Birdie send Claire a look that told him this kind of thing was common. Expectations and reality meeting and clashing.

Finally, Claire turned and noticed Matt, and he saw her stiffen. "Oh, hi. I didn't realize you were here. Everything okay with Sparkle?"

He nodded. "I could use more training treats," he said, holding up the four pouches he'd picked up from the wall display.

She nodded. "I'd better get Tucker back to his kennel."

"Can I follow you? I'd like to say hi to ole Hank, maybe walk him if that's all right?"

Birdie smiled. "He'd love that."

Did Claire just shoot Birdie a look? One that said, *Oh thanks, I wanted to flee his presence*? Yeah, he was pretty sure of it.

He followed Claire down the hallway. She pushed through the door to the Dogs room, Tucker following on his little legs. The dog seemed instantly calmer. He must have gotten used to this area, to the twelve or so big kennels with gated access to the outside—a small fenced area with grass and gravel. This had become home for the pint-size mutt. Matt sure hoped it wouldn't be for too much longer.

Claire put Tucker back in his kennel, and he immediately went to his bed and settled down with his chew toy. Then she joined Matt at Hank's kennel. The big brown dog with the pointy ears was sitting at the front as if he knew Matt was here to take him out for a stroll.

"Hey, ole guy," Matt said, kneeling down, easier this time than yesterday. "How are ya?" He glanced up at Claire. "Can I slip him one of these?" he asked, pulling a treat from the pocket of his leather jacket.

She smiled. "He'd love it." She looked at Hank, her expression clouding up a bit. "A man came in to look at the dogs soon after I started my shift. The guy liked Hank's soulful eyes on his first walk-through of the area, so I brought Hank into the meeting room, hopeful he'd found a match. But he decided he couldn't deal with a three-legged dog. He also didn't like the way Hank's ears didn't flop." She shook her head. "I love Hank's ears."

Matt did too. Seriously, those huge pointy ears almost made Hank look like he could fly by batting them. "Passed up again, huh, guy?" he said, his heart going out to the beautiful dog. "How long has he been here?"

"Almost a month."

"Cooped up here a month? And no one wants him because he's missing a leg and doesn't have floppy ears?" He shook his head. Hell, Hank didn't wince or take fifteen seconds to get up and down the way Matt did with two legs. Hank *ruled*. Hank was the best. Hank was... his? "You know what, Hank? If it's all right with you, I'd like to take you home."

Claire gasped. "Really? That would be amazing!"

Ten seconds ago, he'd had no idea that he wanted to adopt Hank, but he must have wanted to all along. The idea of it was so *right*. He was meant to bring this dog home. Matt wasn't sure of much these days, but he knew that. "Hank's so calm I'm sure he'd be gentle with Sparkle, right?"

"Oh, yes. Those two have played together in the yard a few times since Sparkle first came in. They're great together."

Man, it was nice to see that smile again, such pure joy on Claire's face. Earlier, he'd been responsible for taking it off. Now, he'd put it back.

"Well, if I'm approved to adopt Hank, I'd like to give him a forever home."

"You mean a *fur*ever home," she said with a grin. She wrapped her arms around him and squeezed, then stepped back, her smile fading. "Sorry about that. Just a little excited for one of my favorites. Oh, Matt, I just know you two are a pair."

He held her gaze, her green eyes sparkling. He loved making her so happy. Even if it was about a dog and not the two of them.

And just like that, Matt left with Sparkle's training treats and a whole bunch of other stuff for his new dog, Hank, including a spiffy navy-blue collar and leash, a huge memory foam dog bed, a soft quilt and the toys that Claire said he seemed to like best. A small fortune later, but worth every penny, Matt and Claire had everything in his car, including Hank, who rode shotgun in the front seat. Matt put the passenger-seat window all the way down so Hank could put his face out if he wanted, even in the February chill.

"Your days in a kennel are over, buddy," Matt said, giving Hank a rub along his soft back.

Hank glanced at him in appreciation, Matt could tell, and stuck his snout out the window. The ole guy was smiling. No doubt.

"I could cry, I'm so happy for him," Claire said as she stood in front of the driver's window. "And not only does Hank get a great home, I get to see him all the time!"

Matt gave her a more rueful smile than he'd intended. Seeing each other all the time probably wasn't a good idea. Living in Claire's house probably wasn't a good idea. Hadn't his smart sister said exactly that?

Right now, he was going to focus on getting his new dog settled. He'd think about what the hell he was going to do about Claire Asher later. Much later. Because as much as he knew living on her property was a problem, he didn't want to leave.

BigReader, aka Connor Hearon, was as attractive as his photo had indicated. Tall and lanky, with a mop of light brown hair and warm brown eyes, he gave her hope that she could find another man besides Matt Fielding attractive and interesting. Of course, Matt was on her mind. Taking over her mind, actually. When Connor mentioned he was reading a certain biography, Claire's first thought was that Matt would love the book about a climb up Mt. Everest, since he'd loved reading adventure memoirs as a teenager. When Connor ordered the Main Street Grille's special pasta entrée, Claire thought about how Matt would have gone for that too.

What. Was. Wrong. With. Her?

She knew what. Matt Fielding had adopted Hank. A three-legged senior dog that no one else had wanted. Who'd been languishing at Furever Paws for a month. And he'd adopted him despite already fostering and training a puppy for his niece. So, no matter what Matt said, his actions spoke louder to her soul than his words did to her brain. Did that even make any sense? It did to her heart, unfortunately.

He told you! He's leaving town! He's got some crazy notion stuck in his head that he's not good enough for you, that he has nothing to offer you. That all he has in this world is a duffel bag. And now a dog.

She let herself remember him telling her all that. She *made* herself remember how he'd stopped them from ending up in bed—twice.

And then she forced herself to pay more attention to Connor and push Matt from her consciousness. She focused on the outdoorsman crinkles on the sides of those kind, intelligent eyes.

You know who else has a dog? This guy. BigReader. A man whose profile had stated that he wanted a long-term relationship leading to marriage and children.

"So you're divorced?" Connor asked, twirling his fork in his pasta.

"It's been three years," she said, then bit into her black bean burger. "But I just entered the dating world about six months ago. Ready to get back out there and all."

He nodded. "I've been out there for the past six months too. Eye-opening, huh?"

She smiled. "Well, this is actually my first attempt at online dating. I've been saying yes to fix-ups, but I thought I'd start engineering my own future."

"Fix-ups have gone more my way," he said. "I've noticed a lot of women fib about this or that. Like weight." He puffed out his cheeks.

Uh, really? Did he just say that? *Do* that? "Well, I've heard men post ten-year-old photos of themselves when they had more hair."

BigReader had a head full of hair, so it wasn't as though she was insulting him. Their conversation had taken a bit of a sharp turn, so she wanted to direct it back to kinder, gentler territory.

He seemed to realize that he was being a jerk. "Sorry. I don't mean you. You could probably stand to gain a good five pounds," he added, eyeing her breasts.

Get. Me. Out. Of. Here.

"Oh God, I'm really blowing this, aren't I?" He chuckled, because apparently that was hilarious. "I guess I'm just a little gun-shy about relationships. My last girlfriend was two-timing me. And the girlfriend before that was in it because she thought I made a pot of money." He snorted.

Jeez, couldn't he talk about movies or waterways he'd boated down?

She'd finish her dinner and make an excuse to leave immediately. "Well, at least you have that gorgeous dog, right?" she said, swiping a fry through ketchup. She recalled his profile pic with the majestic golden retriever sitting beside him on the boat. "It's amazing how much joy dogs bring to people's lives. When you're feeling down or you're under the weather, a warm nose and furry body next to you can be so comforting."

He snorted again—this time with a bitter edge. "I lost the dog in the divorce. More like I had no problem letting the ex have Banjo so I could demand what I really wanted. Worked like a charm."

Jerk.

He slurped his pasta, and there was no way she could sit there another second. Just when she was thinking of how she could end this date before he even finished his meal, her friend Amanda came over to the table. "How is everything?"

Claire knew Amanda pretty well since they'd spent many hours together at Furever Paws, and she could see the slight raise of her eyebrow—the question was more directed at how Claire thought the *date* was going.

BigReader held up a finger and made a show of finishing chewing. "The pasta's great, but, honestly? I didn't love the dressing on my salad. I like my Italian a little more…something."

"I'm sorry to hear that," Amanda said, her blue eyes on Connor. "I hope a complimentary dessert will make you forget all about that salad dressing. We have some great offerings tonight—"

"Gotta watch my figure for the online dating thing," he said on a laugh.

Amanda offered Claire a rueful smile, clearly able to see for herself how this date was going, then headed to another table.

"So," Connor said. "Back to your place for a nightcap?"

"I don't think we're a match," Claire replied honestly.

He shrugged again. "No worries. It's a numbers game. You gotta be in it to win it, right?"

Claire just wanted to be out of there. "Being in it isn't easy. It's hard sitting across from someone you have little in common with and didn't know yesterday when there are so many expectations."

"Well, there's your problem, Claire. Expectations. If you're attracted, great. A little making out, even sex. If you're not attracted, buh-bye. Next."

"Well, I guess it's *next* then."

"With that attitude, you'll be single for the rest of your life." He got up and put a twenty-dollar bill on the table, which would barely cover his entrée, his two beers and his share of the tip. "Good luck out there. You'll need it."

"You too," she said, shaking her head, as BigReader made his exit.

"Good riddance to bad date-ish," Amanda said, sliding a slice of chocolate cake in front of Claire. "Compliments of the Main Street Grille for putting up with that guy for an hour."

Claire laughed. And dug in. But now what? How many of these dates was she supposed to go on? If it really *was* a numbers game, she didn't have the energy to date that many frogs to find someone close to a prince. Maybe she should stop forcing it. Let it happen naturally, organically. She had met a few single men while volunteering at Furever Paws, but sharing a love of dogs didn't necessarily mean they'd have much else in common. There was always the upcoming regional teachers conference, which might be a source of potential Mr. Rights. The local parks were full of them too. Joggers. Dog walkers. Bench readers. So she wasn't completely a hopeless case. Except maybe when it came to one man.

The man who refused to be Mr. Right was probably in her own backyard right now with his two pooches. She wanted to be home more than anything else in the world. But since her plan to distract herself from Matt's magnetic pull was a big bust, how was she going to protect her heart against him?

Matt had already taken a thousand pictures of Sparkle being cute, texting them to his sister to share with his niece, but now he had the photo of all photos. Hank, his big body curled up in his memory foam bed, the little brown-and-white puppy nestled alongside his belly.

Laura sent back an aww! and said Ellie was dying to come over to meet Hank and work with Sparkle—how about tomorrow?—so he set that up. After a month in the shelter, Hank deserved getting special fuss treatment from an eight-year-old dog enthusiast.

He glanced at the time on his phone—eight forty-five. "Come on, lazybones," he said to the pooches. "Let's go outside, and then you can curl right back up."

All he had to do to communicate his intentions was pick up a leash. Hank ambled over, Sparkle trotting beside him and giving his one front leg a sniff. Matt put on his leather jacket, eager for the days when he wouldn't have to shiver outside at night, and brought the dogs out. Hands in his pockets, he stood at the far end of the yard, away from Claire's patio. The lights were off inside, and he wondered where she was. *Date?*

Don't think about it, he told himself. The dogs did their business, so he threw a ball for them, Hank flying after it, Sparkle on his heels. Wow, Hank could run well on three legs. He was so much bigger and faster than Sparkle that he got the ball before her every time.

He heard a car pull into the driveway on the other side of the house. Claire. He listened for the front door opening and closing, then saw lights flick on inside. The sliding glass door to the yard opened, and she came out with Dempsey. He couldn't help noticing she was dressed up. And wearing makeup, similar to how she'd looked when he'd run into her on her date with Slick. Both "dog shelter Claire," with a fresh-scrubbed face, ponytail and old jeans, and "date Claire" were stunning.

"Date?" he asked before he could tell his brain not to spit it out.

"Actually, yes." She threw a ball for Dempsey, who was too busy sniffing—and being sniffed by—Hank. The three dogs were moving in a comical circle of sniffing noses, bellies and butts, then stopping to stare off at some unseen critter before resuming their nose work.

"Find Mr. Right?" he asked, his chest tightening.

Why the hell was he even going there? He didn't want to have this conversation.

"He used the dog as a pawn in his divorce to get what he wanted from his ex. She could have the dog, which he said he didn't want anyway, so he could get x, y, z. God, I hate people."

"*Some* people," he said. "You have the right to hate me, Claire. But I hope you don't. You—" *Shut up*, he told himself, clamping his lips shut. He threw a ball for the dogs, and this time they all went for it, Dempsey winning.

"I what?" she asked with something of a wince. He hated that he made her brace herself.

"You once made me want to be a better person," he said. "Yeah, I enlisted in tribute to my brother and to serve my country, but I also knew the army would give me direction—turn me into a good man."

She shoved her hands in her pockets, and suddenly he was aware again of how cold it was. "You were a perfectly good young man in high school," she said.

He shook his head. "I wasn't. You had a thing for me, so you didn't really care that I was barely scraping by in my classes or got into fights with bullies who liked to pick on those who wouldn't or couldn't fight back. I might have been sticking up for kids, but I got sent to the principal and suspended to the point that one more suspension would have gotten me expelled."

"Not everyone is academically oriented," she said. "And how terrible that you stood up for the underdogs. What a terrible person you were, Matthew Fielding."

A rush of dread filled his lungs. She didn't get it. "I had nothing back then and I have nothing now, Claire."

"Then why do I like you so much?" she asked. "Then *and* now? Huh? Answer that."

"Because you're romanticizing old times. Because I seem like some kind of hero for taking in that spinning pup and calming her down, and for adopting Hank, who's the coolest dog in the world. No medal deserved there."

"You're consistent," she said. "I'll give you that."

"The truth is the truth. I am exactly who I appear to be."

"I know," she said, shaking her head, but there was a hint of a smile on her pretty face. "So, it pays to know the owner of the Main Street Grille. Amanda, who also volunteers at Furever Paws, gave me an extra slice of chocolate layer cake in a doggie bag for my 'awesome new tenant who adopted Hank.' That's you."

"But it's a doggie bag, so shouldn't these guys have it?"

She did smile this time. "You know full well that chocolate is toxic for dogs, so it's all ours. I'll give them each a peanut butter treat for welcoming Hank so nicely."

He guessed that meant he was going inside her house, having that slice of cake, continuing this too-personal conversation. He could—and would—turn it back to dogs.

She called the dogs to follow her, and they all trooped inside, Matt glad to get Claire out of the cold. In the kitchen, Claire gave them all treats, and then Dempsey showed Hank around the house, Sparkle at their heels.

All three dogs ended up sitting in front of the door to the deck, staring out at night critters no one could detect.

"This cake is really something," Claire said, setting the slice on a plate and placing it on the kitchen table. She took two beers out of the refrigerator and slid one beside the cake.

Matt took a bite. Mmm, chocolate heaven. "This was thoughtful of you."

She took a sip of beer. "Well, you did a very thoughtful thing."

He raised an eyebrow. "Ah, you mean adopting Hank."

"It's a big deal," she said. "We were really worried he'd never find a home, and then, whammo, the perfect owner and home presents itself."

"I'm hardly perfect. And I don't have a home, Claire. Again, again, again, you make me out to be something I'm not."

"Or you just don't see yourself the way I do. The way a lot of people do."

"Were you always this bossy and stubborn?" he asked, then took another forkful of cake. "Oh, wait, you were." He smiled.

She smiled back at him. "So enough about us, tell me about you. How did your first few hours with Hank go?"

"Great. He's so calm. And even though Sparkle has mellowed a lot from when I took her in, I think Hank is even more of a calming influence on her. Nothing throws him. A slammed door, a pot lid dropping. He's unflappable. And did you see the way he can chase a ball? He's amazing."

She scooched her chair close and kissed him on the cheek, then threw her arms around him.

And, oh hell, it felt so good that he wrapped his arms around her and tilted up her chin. "I want to kiss you more than anything right now." He wasn't going to deny himself this. The pull was too strong. The need too great.

"Be my guest," she said, puckering up.

He laughed. "How am I supposed to kiss you when I'm laughing?"

"Like this," she said, covering his lips with hers, the softness making him melt into a puddle on the chair. Everything about her was soft and smelled like spicy flowers. He couldn't get close enough.

"Want the rest of the cake?" he asked.

"No. I just want more of you," she said.

"Good." He scooped her up, his leg only slightly bothering him, and followed her directions to her bedroom, laying her down on the bed.

In seconds, her dress was over her head and in a heap on the floor, along with his shirt and pants. She kissed a trail along his neck and collarbone, her hands all over his chest and pushing down at the waistband of his boxer briefs.

"You're sure?" he whispered. "Despite everything?"

"I'm sure," she whispered back. She pulled open the drawer of her bedside table and took out a box of condoms. "These might be a few years old."

He found the expiration date. "These are actually good until *tomorrow*."

Surprise lit her green eyes. "Meant to be, then."

He didn't know about that.

But he couldn't resist Claire. Not tonight. Not for another moment. Being with her felt so good, made him feel good about himself, even if afterward...

She said she was sure. She wanted to be taken at her word, had told him to stop making decisions for her, so maybe he really could let himself have this. Tonight. With Claire. Hell, maybe she was right, and it would get him out of her system and she could move on. And he would leave Spring Forest, headed for who knew where, Hank beside him, to start fresh.

Her hands were all over his back, in his hair, and then the boxer briefs were being pushed down. He undid her lacy black bra, inhaling that light perfume in her lush cleavage, and then her hands moved lower, and he lost all ability to think. Finally, eighteen years after meeting Claire, Matt made love to the only woman he'd ever loved.

Chapter Seven

He was gone before she woke up, and as a teacher, Claire woke up at the crack of dawn.

Which meant he'd sneaked away in the middle of the night, unable to deal with the aftermath.

Ah, there was a note on her bedside table, sticking out under her phone.

C—Have early plans, didn't want to wake you.
Took the dogs out, Dempsey too. See you later.
—M

Who had plans at 6:00 a.m.? No one, that's who. Plans to get away, maybe.

That was fine. Listen when someone tells you who they are and how they're going to hurt you. Wasn't that one of her many mottoes? Matt Fielding had made his intentions clear. And so she couldn't fault him for not spooning her all night and then waking her up with kisses along her shoulder, whispering sweet every-things in her ear. There was no everything. There was no anything!

That's fine, she repeated, getting out bed, grateful, at least, that she didn't have to open the deck door to let Dempsey out in the winter chill. A dog walker came every weekday at noon to let Dempsey out and throw a ball for her, and Claire had thought about asking Matt if he'd do that when he took out Sparkle and Hank at midday, but it was probably better that he didn't have a key to her house.

Sigh. At least the sex was amazing, she thought as she went into the bathroom and turned on the shower. *Amazing*. Being with Matt was everything she'd always imagined and more.

But he was leaving town after he finished training Sparkle.

Just keep your heart out of it, and you'll be okay. He'd done the shelter two big favors by fostering one dog and adopting another. He'd done her body a big favor by making her feel like liquid. Granted, she was all hunched and tense now, but it was worth it.

Her head set on straight, Claire got ready for work, with her heart only slightly sunk. By the time she ar-rived at the middle school, her mind was on her stu-dents—a welcome distraction, as they demanded so much from her in so many ways. They were reading the novel *Wonder*, which had every one of them fully engaged, and the day was spent on projects related to the book's themes of inclusion, acceptance and the power of friendship.

After the dismissal bell rang for the end of the school day, Claire graded quizzes and killed some time tidying her up her desk to avoid going home before Divorce Club—which was the pet name for the "book" club she belonged to. Two teachers at the middle school had started it, but when they discovered that all four members were divorced, talk had quickly turned from the book they were supposed to read to their lives and marriage and divorce. They met at a different member's house every two weeks. The meeting didn't start till four thirty, but Claire didn't want to go home and run into Matt. She just wasn't ready to see him or listen to his excuses or however he'd awkwardly explain his disappearing act.

Ah. Finally time. Claire drove over to Danielle Peterwell's house, which was near the area where Claire had grown up. She took a detour of a few blocks to drive past the house she'd lived in with her parents and Della and various dogs over the years. Nostalgia gripped her, and she sat there in her car for a few minutes, until a woman came out of the house with a baby in a carrier and a little boy. The boy scampered across the lawn for a few seconds—like Sparkle, Claire thought with a half smile—then she watched the woman put the carrier into the car and help buckle the boy into his seat.

Huh. Maybe the universe was trying to tell her something by having her stop here. Being all hung up on Matt wasn't going to get her that baby and little boy and a partner to share her life with.

She lifted her chin and drove over to Danielle's, determined to keep her head on straight—and on what she wanted most of all: a family.

At Divorce Club, the members all said their hellos and attacked the very nice spread the hostess had set out: miniquiches, fruit and a light sangria.

"Now last time, I'm pretty sure Claire had a blind date set up by her sister?" Jen Garcia said. "Do tell," she added, taking a sip of sangria.

She'd almost forgotten all about that guy—Andrew something. The lawyer her sister had fixed her up with. Two dates ago. "It actually started out pretty well, but he basically told me at the end of the date that he'd hooked up with his ex the night before."

"He randomly told his blind date that?" Lara Willkowski asked. "Idiot."

"Well, I kind of saw an old boyfriend at the restaurant," Claire admitted, "and when the date asked if I wanted to go for a drink after dinner, I told the truth about being sort of distracted."

"Date fail," Danielle said with a grin.

"Hey, wait," Lara said. "Was the old boyfriend Matt Fielding? From high school?"

Claire nodded and slugged some sangria.

Lara plucked a miniquiche from the tray. "I thought I recognized him. I saw him in the park the other day with an adorable little puppy."

"He's fostering the pup for his sister while he trains her. Sparkle's a gift for his young niece."

"Wow, *that's* nice of him," Danielle said pointedly. The group knew how passionate Claire was about

Furever Paws. "And yesterday he adopted a ten-year-old, three-legged dog named Hank," Claire said. "I'm sunk."

She wasn't going to mention last night. She basically had to forget it herself.

"And…?" Jen prompted.

Claire shrugged. "We're kind of on different paths."

Luckily, Danielle started talking about how she and the first guy she dated after her divorce were on different paths too, to the point that he moved to Nepal to climb very tall mountains. Which led to a conversation change to outdoorsy men who liked to hike when Danielle just wanted to go out to lunch or dinner and wear cute shoes. Jen, who loved to hike, had had a date with a couch potato the other night, and they were both willing to give it another try.

But there was nothing to *try* when it came to Matt. Claire just had to accept that they were in two very different places in their lives and looking for different things. She had to let him go.

Even after that glorious sex. Even after feeling so close to him that while he was making love to her, she kept thinking: *this is what homecoming feels like.*

Keep it together, Claire, she ordered herself. *Don't get all emotional right now.* The Divorce Club crew was great and would rally around her, but she didn't want the focus to be on herself.

She thought about what her late mother had told her when she was struggling in the aftermath of her divorce. *You sit with how you feel, and you accept that you're heartbroken. You don't have to pretend to feel fine. Just let yourself feel what you feel and grieve. It's all part of the process.*

Now, she'd take that good advice again and let herself sit with her feelings about Matt, though her emotions were all over the place, her thoughts about the situation ping-ponging as if Dempsey and Hank had the rackets. She'd always loved Matt and always would.

And unfortunately, last night, she'd fallen deeper.

"So do you think there's a chance you and Matt could pick up where you left off?" Danielle asked as she set out the dessert tray; four slices of cherry cheesecake. Claire was going to eat every ounce of that cake, despite the chocolate cake she'd had last night. In fact, she would probably let herself have all the decadent desserts she wanted this entire week.

"Only in my fantasies," Claire said.

"You never know," Jen said, forking a piece of cheesecake. "That's become my new motto."

But Claire *did* know. Unless she wanted to break her own heart this time, she'd keep her emotional distance from Matt Fielding.

Using a high-backed chair for support, Matt did the exercises his new physical therapist had had him do this morning. Zeke Harper, an old buddy from town, whom he'd run into at the park a few weeks ago while teaching Sparkle the *come* command, had recommended him. Zeke knew the guy from volunteering at a veterans' center, and had mentioned that Matt still had some stiffness from his IED injury. The guy had offered to work with Matt free of charge, but could only fit him in at 7:00 a.m. The workout had hurt but had felt good. Just like now.

When he'd woken up in Claire's bed this morning, he'd almost been amazed it hadn't been a dream. He'd lain there, also aware that for the first time in months, he hadn't had a nightmare about the day he'd been injured, the day that had sent him home. He'd opened his eyes to find Hank sitting at the edge of the bed, staring at him with those soulful, amber-colored eyes. Sparkle and Dempsey, meanwhile, were curled in Dempsey's dog bed on the other side of the bedroom.

And then there was Claire. His beautiful Claire, whose face and voice and memory had seen him through the worst of his recuperation, like an angel. He'd never expected to run into her in Spring Forest; he'd never imagined in a million years she'd still be in their old hometown. And then he woke up in her bed, naked, next to a naked Claire.

He shouldn't have touched her, but maybe she was right about them getting each other out of their systems.

Not that that was working yet. He'd thought of little else all day but how good last night was, how comfortable and natural and right. He had to keep reminding himself to keep things on a physical level, to keep emotions out of it.

Because he was leaving. Probably sometime in mid- to late March, a few weeks, six at most, he figured. Sparkle was coming along so well in her training that she'd be good to go very soon. Ellie had come over after school today as planned, and Matt had taught her what he knew. If Ellie thought he walked on water before, now she looked at him with wonder and called him the Dog Prince.

That had made him laugh. Matt Fielding, anyone's prince. Even a dog's.

"Right, Hank?" he asked, giving the old guy a belly rub. Hank immediately stretched out his long body so that Matt wouldn't stop. "Maybe I am the Dog Prince. Or do I have that backward?" he asked, giving Hank a vigorous rub. "You're the best, dude," he said.

Hank just stared at him, but Matt knew the dog could understand him.

A car pulled into the driveway, which told him Claire was home. He owed her an explanation for leaving the way he did that morning. After the night they'd shared. Despite the note, he had to say *something*.

He heard her deck door open, so he went down the stairs to the yard. The weather had turned colder, just above freezing, and she stood there, her arms wrapped around her coat.

"Hey," he said as she reached the bottom landing. He should have put on gloves. He shoved his hands in the pockets of his leather jacket.

She glanced over at him. "Hi." She threw a ball for Dempsey, who went flying after it.

"I just wanted to explain why I left so early," he said, looking everywhere but at her.

"No need. You've made yourself clear, Matt. You don't owe me explanations. And I don't regret last night. Not a single second of it. And that includes you leaving at the crack of dawn. Last night was a long time coming."

He tilted his head. "Yes, it was."

"Well, it's freezing out here, so I'm going to get Dempsey back inside."

He nodded, wishing he could go with her, wishing for a repeat of last night, wishing again that things were different, that he had a future to offer her.

As she opened the sliding glass door and Dempsey scooted through, he said, "Claire?"

She turned.

"Did it work? Did you get me out of your system?"

She looked at him for a moment. "No."

Neither did I, he thought as she disappeared inside. *Neither did I.*

Claire avoided Matt the following week, which was difficult since she always waited until he came back in with his dogs early in the morning before taking Dempsey out. She wished things weren't so strained between them. She missed Sparkle and Hank. And Matt's niece, Ellie, had been over twice after school when Claire had gotten home. She'd wanted more than anything to join them in the yard to watch Matt teach Ellie training tips. But she'd stayed inside.

Ugh. This wasn't what she wanted. But in a month, he'd leave in that black Mustang and she'd be here, living the same old life, just like the one she'd had before he'd come back. Except she honestly didn't think she could do that. His return had changed something in the air, changed *her,* and when he was gone, there was no way in hell she was going on bad date after bad date to find her life partner and the father of the child she wanted so badly.

"I should just devote my life to dogs," she said to

Dempsey, running her hand over the fur on the dog's back and sides. She got a lick on the hand for that. As usual, Dempsey seemed to know when she needed comfort and curled up beside her on the couch, her head on Claire's thigh. "Dogs are not confusing like certain tall, dark and very good-looking humans."

On Saturday morning, Claire woke up early to head over to Furever Paws for the weekend adoption event. She would be walking Dempsey around the shelter with an Adopt Me! banner draped over her back. These events brought a lot of visitors to the property, so the staff and volunteers typically walked a few dogs around that they wanted to highlight. The other dogs were kept in their kennels, because the large number of people, with their strange smells and grabbing hands, could be stressful for them.

"Hi, Claire," Bunny said, putting the banner over Cutie Pie, the shepherd mix she'd been fostering.

Claire smiled at Bunny. "Everything set for the event?"

Bunny nodded, surveying Cutie Pie and grabbing a red bandanna from the display wall. She tied it around the dog's neck. "There. Now you're ready for your close-up." She straightened and glanced around, then leaned close to Claire. "Isn't Matt with you?"

Claire raised an eyebrow. "Matt is most definitely not with me. Why would he be?"

Bunny headed over to the desk where two volunteers were stacking adoption applications, foster applications, and information packets. "He called last night and asked if we could use some extra help for the adoption event. I said of course."

Why was Matt so damn helpful except when it came to their relationship?

"We got some very promising applications online for four dogs and six cats," Birdie said as she came in from the back hallway. "I've approved three for the dogs and four for the cats. One of the rejected cat applicants thought her already thirteen black cats might like another now that they're bored of each other." She rolled her eyes. "And the other one has a dog who hates cats but would surely learn to love pretty, long-haired Glenda."

Claire shook her head. "Well, good for the ones who passed muster." She knew the dog adoption applications would require a home visit, but if everything checked out, those dogs would be going to their forever homes. "I guess Dempsey wasn't among them?"

"Sorry," Birdie said. "I don't know why she keeps being passed up." She bent down and petted Dempsey. "You're a beautiful, sweet dog and someone is going to snatch you up soon. Mark my words."

There was a knock at the door. The shelter wasn't open yet, so it had to be a volunteer without a key. Matt.

Yup, there he was. Looking gorgeous in his black leather jacket, jeans and work boots. He greeted Birdie and Bunny and nodded at Claire. She nodded back.

"How can I help?" he asked.

Birdie set him to work hanging Adoption Event banners on the upper walls. As more volunteers and foster parents came in with their dogs, Claire lost track of Matt. Then she spotted him standing near the door with Birdie, who'd handed him a stack of information packets so that he could greet each potential adopter with all the info they needed on the available dogs and cats.

The morning passed in a whirlwind of activity. So many people came through the doors. Seven cats found new homes, and the four preapproved applicants for the dogs had all confirmed they wanted the dogs they'd fallen for online now that they'd met them in person. Two volunteers would do home checks today, and then the adoptions would be made official.

"I keep seeing Dempsey's profile on your website and clicking on it," a woman said to Claire, bending to pet Dempsey, who sat beside her. "I just love her coloring. Like my hair," she added on a laugh.

"Like cinnamon," Claire agreed, though she didn't think it was much of a reason to be drawn to a dog. Or maybe it was. People fell in love for all kinds of reasons.

"She's awfully big, though," the woman added, giving Dempsey a pat. "Aren't you, you big thing," she singsonged in baby talk.

Dempsey eyed the woman as if she were above baby talk, but Claire knew Dempsey loved it. When it came to shelter animals, baby talk was a very welcome thing.

After answering the woman's many questions, Claire asked if she'd like to fill out an application.

"I don't know," the woman said. "I was thinking of a much smaller dog. A cuter dog, you know? Not that Dempsey isn't cute. She's just so…boxer-y."

Sigh. "Well, she is a boxer mix."

This woman sounded all wrong for Dempsey. Like she'd maybe take her and then return her two weeks later. "You know what? Dempsey is beautiful, and I always seem to come back to her. So, maybe I can take her for a walk outside and see how it goes?"

Claire set her up with a leash and led the woman to

the fenced yard. She stood by the door while the woman walked Dempsey. At least the prospective adopter was affectionate, giving Dempsey lots of TLC.

"I'd like to put in an application," the woman said when she returned.

Claire expected to be elated, but instead her heart felt like it weighed two thousand pounds. Granted, Dempsey's potential new mom was a bit wishy-washy, but adopting a dog was a big decision. Better to talk it out than be impulsive.

"Great," Claire said, handing the woman an application. "Why don't you take a seat here and fill it out." She gestured at the rectangular table that Matt had set up in the lobby with chairs and a canister of pens. "Then I'll go over it and pass it to one of the owners for final approval."

"Could that happen today? I was planning to binge-watch season two of my favorite show on Netflix, and I'd hate to have to be interrupted to walk her, especially in the cold."

Oh brother. *You can watch your shows anytime. Bringing home a new dog is a special occasion.* Claire frowned and rubbed Dempsey's side. "Well, we'll see," was all she would and could say.

As the woman got busy filling out the application, Claire put Dempsey into one of the kennels with a chew toy. "I'll be back for you, I promise." A strange feeling was lodged in her stomach, something she couldn't quite identify.

"Crazy day," a familiar voice said.

Matt. She locked Dempsey's kennel and stood up.

"Someone put in an application for Dempsey. I can't believe it. She might have a permanent home."

"Looking good?" he asked.

Claire shrugged. "Hard to tell. People sometimes say nutty things when they're in unfamiliar territory. She'd be a first-time dog owner. I guess I need to give her the benefit of the doubt until I read through her application."

"Miss?" called a high-pitched voice. "Miss?"

Claire glanced out the window and down the hallway, toward the voice. The woman who wanted to adopt Dempsey was standing and waving at her. "Guess her application is ready."

Matt gave her a gentle smile. "I'm not quite sure if you want Dempsey to be adopted or not."

"Of course I want her to be adopted," she snapped. "I've fostered twenty-one dogs since I started volunteering here. Giving them up to the right home is the point." Her voice was sharper than she'd intended, and she let out a breath. "Sorry. Didn't mean to take your head off. Dempsey is special. I just want her to be in the right home."

"Understood," he said, putting a hand on her shoulder, and it felt so good, so comforting that she wanted him to pull her against him and hold her tight.

She'd always known she'd have to say goodbye to Dempsey someday. Same with Matt. The two in the same time frame? That, she wasn't so sure she could bear.

But she sucked in a breath and left the Dogs room to go read over the application belonging to Dempsey's potential adopter, her legs like lead.

Chapter Eight

Claire held Gwyneth Cardle's application for Dempsey and read each line carefully. The woman lived in a single-family home, but there was no fenced yard.

"Since you don't have a fenced yard, are you prepared to walk Dempsey at least three times a day, for taking care of business and exercise?"

"Three times?" Gwyneth said, her eyes popping. "I'm figuring on walking her right before I leave for work at eight thirtyish, and then when I get home at five thirty."

Claire stared at her. "You realize that's nine hours."

"She's a big dog, though. I read that big dogs can hold it longer."

Claire marked an *X* next to Residence Information.

"So, Dempsey will be alone for nine hours each

weekday?" Claire asked. "No contact with people or dogs and no potty break or exercise?"

"I work," the woman snapped. "So sue me."

"You could hire a dog walker to come at noon," Claire said. "I work and that's what I do."

"Not everyone can afford that," Gwyneth muttered. "She'll have to hold it in."

Claire marked an *X* next to Understands Dogs' Needs and went over the rest of her application, which was as dismal. Under the area that asked what provisions she would make for the dog if she went on vacation, Gwyneth had written: "I really don't know."

Next.

If there would be a next. *Looks like you're mine a bit longer, Dempsey*, she thought, a feeling she recognized all too well as relief washing over her.

"Thanks so much for filling out the application and for your interest in Dempsey," she said to Gwyneth. "I'll pass the application to one of the shelter owners, and we'll be in touch by the end of the day."

"Could you not call before five?" she asked, putting on her jacket. "I'm planning on watching five episodes of my show today, so…"

Claire mentally rolled her eyes. "Well, one of the Whitaker sisters will contact you via email. So, no worries."

As Claire watched the woman walk away and stick her finger in an adoptable kitten's kennel in the lobby, despite the big sign that read: Please Do Not Put Fingers in Kennels, she thought about how satisfying it would be to stamp the application with Not Recommended.

On her way to the desk to do just that, Claire's phone pinged with a text. Jasmine, one of her teacher friends from the middle school.

Help! Babysitter canceled and tonight's my brother-in-law's wedding. Can you take Tyler? Six to midnightish.

Ooh. Tyler was a precious, adorable, baby-shampoo-scented seven-month-old with huge brown eyes and a gummy smile.

She texted back, Of course! I'll come pick him up so you don't get baby spit-up on the gorgeous dress I'm sure you're wearing.

Thank you!!! I owe you BIG.

Clare smiled. *Au contraire.* She loved babysitting, especially babies.

And what better way to try to get Matt out of her system than to focus on what she wanted for herself: a child.

That night, as Matt took Sparkle and Hank into the yard, he could have sworn he saw Claire walking back and forth in her living room with a baby in her arms. Seeing things?

Nope. Because there she was again. Walking and patting the baby on the back.

He swallowed. How many nights had he thought about "what might have been?" if he and Claire had married. Had children. Sometimes he'd think of them with a baby, sometimes with six kids. And then the images would fade because *come on*. Matt Fielding, someone's father? A thirty-six-year-old man with a duffel bag and a three-legged dog to his name?

He could see Dempsey staring forlornly out the glass door, hoping to be let out to play with her friends. But Claire clearly had her hands full and looked a bit exasperated.

As she looked out and spotted him, he quickly held up a hand and came over to the door. She slid it open just a bit since she obviously didn't want to let the cold air inside to chill the baby.

"I'll take Dempsey if it's easier on you," he said.

"Oh, thank God," she sputtered. "I love Tyler to pieces, but he's been crying for half an hour. He was fine when I picked him up from my colleague's house."

"So you're babysitting for the night?" he asked.

She nodded, rocking the baby in her arms. "It's okay, little guy," she cooed to the baby. "Everything is okay."

A bell dinged, and Claire glanced toward the left. "Oh crud. That's my oven timer. Could you hold Tyler for just a minute while I get the cookies out of the oven?"

What? She wanted him to hold the baby? The squawking, red-faced baby?

"Matt?" she asked. "I don't want to just put him down in his bouncer while he's so miserable."

"Okay," he said, stepping inside the living room and closing the sliding glass door behind him. He held out his arms, clueless as to how to take a baby, let alone hold one. She handed the baby over, and maybe it was the change of scenery of his face versus Claire's, but the baby stopped crying. Matt took him under the arms and cradled him against his chest, finding that holding the tot was just sort of instinctive. "Name's Matt," he said to the baby.

Claire burst out laughing from the kitchen. She poked her head out of the kitchen doorway. "Oh God, I needed that. Thank you." She poked her head back in and continued laughing.

"Something funny about what I said?" he asked, eyes narrowed toward the kitchen, from where the smell of warm cookies emanated.

She came back inside the living room, grinning. "Yes, actually. 'Name's Matt,'" she said, making her voice deeper. She chuckled and reached out to caress the baby's face.

"Well, shouldn't I introduce myself?"

"You don't spend much time around babies, do you?" she asked.

"Nope. But look at me now? Baby whisperer." He rocked the baby a bit as he had seen Claire do earlier. Tyler laughed.

Matt's mouth dropped open. "He laughed! Babies laugh?"

"They sure do. And he sure seems to like you. You *are* the baby whisperer."

"Whodathunk," he said, moving to the couch to sit down. Tyler immediately grabbed his chin.

"The dogs are all right on their own?" he asked.

Claire went to the glass door and peered out. "Hank appears to be overseeing the other two as he gnaws on a rope toy. Sparkle is sniffing under the tree, and Dempsey is digging in the spot I made for her to do just that."

"So, since you're babysitting and not bringing Dempsey to her new home, I assume that woman's application didn't work out."

"She thought leaving a dog home alone for nine hours every weekday was no big deal," Claire said. "I mean, maybe some dogs can handle that but it's not ideal. Given that she didn't seem a good match for Dempsey in most ways, I didn't recommend her."

"Well, I'm sure the right person will come along. Just like me for Hank."

She stared at him, and he wondered if she was applying that statement to herself, as well.

Tyler gripped Matt's ear and pulled with a squeal of joy.

"Ow," Matt said on a laugh. "Quite an arm you got there." He tickled the baby's belly and made funny faces at him, sticking out his tongue.

Tyler laughed that big baby laugh that was almost impossible to imagine coming from such a bitty body.

"You really have a way with babies," Claire said. "Ever think about fatherhood?"

His smile faded. "Of course not."

"Of course not?" she repeated.

"Claire. If I have nothing to offer a woman, I have nothing to offer a baby. I wouldn't inflict myself on an innocent life."

"You really don't see yourself the way others do," she said.

"Key word there is *see*. I know who I am. Others *see* an honorably discharged soldier. They don't look past the uniform and what it represents."

"Because it means so much," she said. "It speaks for itself."

"I didn't say I'm a bad person. Just that I have nothing to offer a family. So I'm not going there."

"Matt, you've been home only a couple of weeks. You expect to have your new life figured out already? I certainly don't expect that of you."

Once again, she just didn't understand. Making a baby laugh didn't mean he was cut out for fatherhood. Training a puppy didn't mean he was cut out for man of the year.

"Claire, do yourself a favor and stop trying to make me into something I'm not. I don't want a wife. I don't want a baby. I'm on my own. Me and Hank."

She stared at him. "I'll never forget you telling me that when you had a son, you were going to name him Jesse, after your brother."

His chest seized up and the back of his eyes stung. He pictured his brother, older by four years, the best person Matt had ever known. And his hero.

"Did I say that?" he managed to choke out.

"Yes, you did," she said softly.

He closed his eyes and got up and put the baby in the bouncer, latching the little harness. He pushed the On button and the bouncer gently swung side to side. He watched Tyler's eyes droop and droop some more until they closed.

"Magic," she said, moving closer behind him.

He turned around and pulled her into a hug. "I did say that," he whispered. A long time ago, but he'd said it.

"And his middle name would be Thomas, after my dad."

He closed his eyes again. He remembered saying that too. She'd lost her father when she was only nine, barely older than Ellie. Then her mother had died a few years ago; he'd heard the news through his sister. "I'm so sorry about your mom. I don't think I ever said that. When my sister mentioned it in a letter, I wanted to write you, but then I thought I should just leave well enough alone."

"I wish you had written," she said. "I wish a lot of things."

He put his hands on either side of her face, and she looked up at him. There was so damned much hovering between them. History and feeling. He lowered his face, and she tilted up even higher to kiss him.

"I'm leaving by the end of March," he said, taking a step back. "Sparkle will be ready for my sister's house. I need to be clear. There's not going to be any baby named Jesse."

She stepped back as if he'd slapped her.

A dog barked, then others chimed in. Matt went to the glass door and looked out, his chest tight, his heart racing. The dogs were standing under a tree, staring up at a fat squirrel racing across one of the branches. "I'd better get these guys out of the cold."

"We all need to be let out of the cold," she said. "The deep freeze."

He glanced at her, then walked over to Tyler. "Night, little guy," he whispered, and then fled outside.

On Sunday afternoon, Claire accompanied Bunny on a home check for a couple who had an approved application to adopt Pierre, a two-year-old black Lab mix they'd met at the adoption event earlier that day. The Changs had an adorable toddler named Mia and lived in a classic white Colonial with a red door. They had a fenced yard, and had already decked out the house with everything a dog could need—plush beds in a few rooms, food and water bowls, toys and two sets of leashes and harnesses, plus an assortment of poop bags. These people were prepared to bring a dog into their family.

"Mia's first word was dog," Camille Chang said, the little girl on her lap.

Bunny smiled. "Well, Mia, I'm happy to let you know that you'll now have a dog of your very own."

"So all is well with the home check?" Michael Chang asked.

"All is well. You can come pick up Pierre anytime." She added her card to Pierre's paperwork, which included the Chang's application. Claire watched her write *Approved to adopt Pierre—Bunny W.* across the back of the card. "Just show this at the desk and he's all yours."

They left the very happy Changs and headed out to Bunny's ancient car with the Furever Paws logo painted on the sides.

Claire got in and buckled up with a deep sigh. When she realized she actually sighed out loud, she winced.

"What's got you all wistful?" Bunny asked. "Spill it."

Claire smiled. "You know when you want something but the someone you want it with isn't interested in any of it, including you, but you want him, and so you're just spinning your wheels in what feels like gravel?"

"I assume you're talking about our handsome new volunteer?"

Claire nodded—and then found herself launching into every detail of her relationship, and lack thereof, with Matt Fielding.

"Ah, well, he's interested all right."

"He's told me flat out he's not. Attracted, yes," she added, thinking she probably should have left out the part about ending up in bed. But the Whitaker sisters were hardly shrinking violets, and she'd always felt she could get personal with them. "Interested in a future with me? A family one day? No."

Bunny turned the ignition. "My hard-won wisdom is this, Claire. He's interested. In fact, he probably just doesn't know how to get from here to there. You've just got to flip him."

Claire raised an eyebrow. "Flip him? What do you mean?"

"You've said he doesn't think he has what it takes to be a husband and a father because he has nothing to offer. But he's shown you time and again he most definitely is husband and daddy material."

"Right," Claire said. "But where does the flipping come in?"

"By spending time with him, not hiding or avoiding

him. The more he sees for himself who he is, the closer you'll get to your dream."

Her dream. Husband, children. Dogs. "Am I that transparent?"

Bunny grabbed Claire's hand and squeezed. "Sorry, but yes. You love that man."

Claire bit her lip. She did.

"So are you going to give up like you had no choice when you were eighteen? Or are you going to make that man yours?"

Claire smiled. "You make it sound so easy."

Bunny backed out of the Changs' driveway and headed toward the shelter. "He adopted Hank, Claire. He's halfway there already. He just doesn't know it."

"Halfway could go either way. Backward or forward," Claire pointed out.

"If you're a pessimist like Birdie, maybe." Bunny chuckled, then added, "Don't tell my sister I said that. She calls herself a *realist*."

"I think I need a dash of you to believe this relationship has a chance, and a dash of Birdie to keep my head out of the clouds."

And she wasn't so sure that adopting Hank meant Matt was setting down roots. Making something his. Creating permanence. Dogs loved unconditionally and didn't talk or ask for much. They were easy to love. People were much harder.

But Bunny was right—Matt's adopting Hank was a major sign of his commitment to love, honor and cherish that living, breathing creature. *A* living, breathing creature. It was a start, and all she had at the moment, so she was going to run with Bunny's dreamer ways.

"Oh, and Claire?" Bunny said as she pulled into Furever Paws' gravel parking lot. "He named his some-day son. I'm not sure you need more *sign* than that."

"That was a long time ago, when he was a different person."

"Was he? According to the broken record of Matt Fielding, he had nothing to offer you then and has nothing to offer now. So for him, nothing is different. If he could imagine being a father then, he could imagine being one now." She smiled and shook her head. "Men."

Huh. Bunny was absolutely right.

Except he was leaving by the end of March. "He's out of here in four weeks, Bunny."

"Or not, dear."

He'd left once. For eighteen years. Claire had no doubt the most stubborn man she'd ever met would do it again.

Chapter Nine

Was Matt really walking the dogs around the front of Claire's house to avoid running into her in the backyard with Dempsey? *Yes.* He sighed, hating that it had come to this. How could he want to be with someone so much and want to avoid her at the same time? What the hell was that?

The front door opened and Dempsey's snout, followed by the rest of her and then Claire, came outside. Guess Claire had the same idea.

Awk-ward.

"Oh, hi," she said.

"Hey."

Dempsey started pulling on her leash, something he didn't think he ever saw her do. Must be a particularly interesting squirrel nearby.

Sparkle started pulling too and barking up a storm. "Whoa there, pup," he said. The only dog not pulling was Hank, but he was staring at something across the road.

Matt glanced toward where they were staring. A small, gray, scruffy dog was half-hiding behind the wheel of a car parked across the street. "See that dog?" he asked Claire. "Sure looks skinny and bedraggled."

Claire gasped. "It's him! I saw him a few days ago and tried to lure him with treats, but he was scared and then a truck passed by and must have spooked him, because he took off running."

"I don't see a collar," Matt said. "Poor thing must be a stray from the looks of him."

"I think so too."

"Here, I'll take Dempsey. Maybe you can lure him over with treats now."

Claire handed over Dempsey and pulled a treat from her pocket. "Here, sweetie," she said, bending down a bit as she moved forward toward the curb. The mutt was still half-hiding, staring at the dogs more than her—or the treat.

"Ruff! Grr-ruff!" Sparkle barked.

"Shh, Sparkle," Matt said. "You might scare him away."

Claire stepped off the sidewalk and onto the street. But just then, a teenager on a moped came racing down the road, and the dog took off running.

Oh no.

Claire ran after him, treat in hand, but then she stopped, throwing her hands up before she came back.

"I lost him. Poor guy. It's so cold at night, especially. I called the animal warden when I saw him a couple of days ago, but she hasn't been able to find him."

"Well, we know he likes this road. So maybe he'll be back."

Claire bit her lip. "I hate the idea of that skinny, hungry little thing out there on his own."

"I know. But let's hope for the best. You'd bring him to the shelter?" he asked.

She nodded. "Our vet, Dr. Jackson—we call him Doc J—would check him out with a full exam, and we'd go from there. The little dog seemed to be in good enough shape."

"I'll keep an eye out," Matt said. "Maybe he'll be back later."

She nodded. "Me too. But little dogs are hard to catch. So many places to hide. I don't want you to be disappointed if we can't rescue him."

"I will be. I know what it's like to think you have nowhere to go." He froze. *What the hell?* He hadn't intended to say that.

"You'll always have somewhere to go, Matt. You have your sister, and no matter what, I'll always be your friend. Even if I'm really, really, really mad at you."

That actually made him smile. "Are you? Mad at me."

"Yeah, I am."

The snapping miniature poodle two doors down was storming down the sidewalk, pulling her owner, who kept saying "One day I'm going to hire a trainer."

"Dempsey's nemesis," Claire said. "I think I'll head back inside. Thanks for holding her."

"Anytime," he said.

The second the door closed behind them, he missed Claire. He really hoped they'd find and rescue that gray dog. Because somehow, in no time at all, Matt had become a dog person. And because he wanted to do something to make Claire happy.

With Dempsey at Doc J's main office for a dental cleaning, Claire's house sure was…lonely. She attempted to bake a pie, which came out lopsided and missing something vital, like sugar, maybe. Then she cleaned both bathrooms and vacuumed Dempsey's fur off all surfaces. She watched two episodes of a TV show, then tried to read a memoir about a woman who adopted a dog after divorce and it changed her life.

But she couldn't concentrate on anything. She kept lifting her eyes to the ceiling and toward the right, wondering what was going on in Matt's over-the-garage apartment. Part of her wanted to march up the deck stairs, knock on that that man's door and tell him straight-up how she felt, point out that he clearly felt something too, and that he was being ridiculous. And that he'd better fall in love with her *this minute*.

Well, maybe she'd just tell him how she felt. He was leaving soon. If his response was, *Sorry, I just don't feel the same way* or more of *I can't because of this-that*, at least she wouldn't be mortified around him for long. But there was a chance she could get through to him. Flip him, like Bunny had suggested.

She went upstairs to her bedroom and sat down at her dressing table, planning to doll herself up a bit, but frowned in the mirror instead. *Take me or leave me. This is who I am. A woman who teaches tweens all day and gets down and dirty with dogs all evening at the shelter. Accept me, dog hair and all.*

She got up, went to the kitchen for a bottle of red wine and a block of one of her favorite cheeses, put on her jacket, then went out the deck door and up the stairs to Matt's entrance. She knocked. *Please don't let me humiliate myself—again*, she thought.

He answered the door with a towel around his waist, damp from the shower and looking so incredibly sexy, she couldn't find words for a moment. Luckily, two sets of canine eyes were staring at her as Sparkle and Hank stood beside him, assessing the interloper. She cleared her throat and gave each a scratch under the chin.

He eyed the wine and cheese with interest in his blue eyes. "What are we celebrating?"

"A second chance for us." She held her breath.

He shook his head. "Claire, you dodged a bullet with me. Why can't you understand that? My life is completely up in the air right now."

"Really? Looks to me like your feet are solidly on the ground. You have a home, family nearby, a *dog*."

He tilted his head. "I *do* have a dog, don't I? Never saw that one coming."

She smiled. "Life is happening, Matt. You might be trying to stand still because being out of the military is a culture shock for you. But life is moving around you, and you're responding whether you mean to or not. Hence, Hank."

"Hence?" He laughed.

"I'm an English teacher. So *hence*. Hence, Matt Fielding, shut up and let what is going to happen happen instead of trying to fight it for reasons that aren't standing up to scrutiny."

He smiled and shook his head. "I guess I could use a glass of wine."

Thank you, universe! she shouted in her head. She went into his kitchen and took out two wineglasses from a cabinet and poured. They clinked. And that was when the towel dropped.

Oh my. She'd seen him naked not too long ago, but oh wow, oh wow, oh wow. Matt Fielding was magnificent. Tall and muscled and strong. She lifted up her face to kiss him.

He kissed her and kissed her and kissed her, and suddenly, he was walking her backward, his lips still on hers, toward the bedroom.

"I can't stop thinking about you," he whispered, his hands in her hair as they stood just inside the doorway. "Everywhere I look, there you are—my apartment, my dogs, my past. I spent an hour searching for that little gray dog mostly to see your smile when I found him."

She was speechless for a moment. She couldn't even process everything he'd just said, so she focused on the easy part. "Did you find him?"

"He slowed down a few blocks from here, and I thought I could stop my car and lure him over with little bits of a mozzarella cheese stick, but something spooked him and he took off. I couldn't find him after that."

"I appreciate that you tried, Matt." She led him by the hand to the bed and kissed him again, slowly sinking down to the edge of the mattress.

This is so right, she thought over and over. *Can't you feel it?* she silently asked him. *There's no way you can't feel this.*

"You know what I think is unfair?" he asked, one hand in her hair, the other undoing a button on her shirt.

"What?"

"That you're still dressed while I'm naked."

She grinned and got rid of her clothes, aware of him watching her remove every last piece of wool and cotton and lace from her body.

"You do, right?" she asked, running her hands over his glorious chest, all hard planes and muscles.

He trailed kisses up her neck, pausing briefly to ask, "Do what?"

"Feel this. What's between us." She could actually feel him freeze, his body just *stop*. "I want you to stay. And I don't mean just the night, Matt. There, I said it. No one's a mind reader, right? Now you know."

He sat up against the headboard, grabbing part of the top sheet to cover him from the waist down. "I can't stay, Claire. And I really don't want to talk about it."

She stood up and quickly dressed. "Let me tell you something, *bub*."

"Bub?" he repeated.

"Yes, *bub*."

"I'm listening," he said.

"What you might not realize is that you actually do have one thing to offer, Matt. And it happens to be the only thing I want from you."

He stared at her. "I can't possibly come up with anything you could be talking about."

"The one thing you have to offer is *yourself*, Matt Fielding."

He shook his head. "Matt Fielding is a shell, Claire."

Grrr! "A shell? Does a shell of a man adopt a senior three-legged dog and buy every treat and toy and dog bed for his comfort? Does a shell of a man foster a nutty puppy for his smitten niece? Does a shell of a man volunteer at an animal shelter and move furniture around the Whitaker sisters' house? You *love*, Matt. Whether you want to admit it or not. You're just choosing to avoid commitment."

"That's where you're wrong. It's not a choice. This thing in here," he said, slapping a hand over his chest, "is blocked by a brick wall. It's there all the time. The dogs, two sixtysomething sisters with nicknames, and an eight-year-old with a crooked braid don't threaten my equilibrium. I'm not looking for attachments beyond them."

She crossed her arms over her chest. "So you're just a lone wolf."

"Better than what you're doing with Dempsey. You're so attached to her, when you're just going to have to let her go. I saw the look on your face, the tension in your body language when she got that application the other day. Loving Dempsey means breaking your own heart."

"Bullcrap. Love is all there is in this crazy world.

Everything you've been through has helped build that brick wall in that chest of yours, but I can help break it down if you'll let me. You have to let someone in, Matt. May as well be me."

Please don't say Sorry *and turn away. Stop pushing me out of your life.*

"I am really sorry, Claire. But I'm leaving in a few weeks as planned."

She could use that brick wall over her own heart right about now. Because it was breaking again, and she was powerless to protect herself. So she did the only thing she could. She left.

After rushing downstairs from Matt's last night, Claire had kept busy by grading quizzes and baking and cleaning some more. At least her house was spotless. She'd spent the night tossing and turning in her bed, vacillating between giving up on Matt as the lost cause he said he was and being on Team Bunny and working on the flip. Which apparently she was no good at.

There was a rap at the sliding glass door. Matt stood there with Sparkles's and Hank's leashes dangling from his neck.

"Hi," she said, barely able to look at him.

"Hi. I just realized I forgot to bring down poop bags. Got two extras?"

Sigh. He could have run up and gotten some from his apartment. She supposed it meant he was trying, that he wasn't avoiding her.

"Come in out of the cold," she said. "I have some in the kitchen."

Just as she rounded the kitchen, her phone dinged with a text. It was from Birdie.

GREAT application just came in for Dempsey! Forwarding to you.

Goose bumps broke out along Claire's spine and arms. And not in a good way, she realized.

She went to her laptop on the kitchen island and opened Birdie's email and the application. Her heart sunk with every line. A single, middle-aged writer, who worked at home, didn't have a fenced yard but lived near wooded trails and would walk Dempsey at least three times a day, who "lost my furbaby last year to cancer and am finally ready to love another dog." She fell in love with Dempsey at the adoption event last week but had wanted to sit with her feelings, and yes, she'd love to have "beautiful, majestic, lovely" Dempsey.

Claire burst into tears, her hands darting up to her face. Her shoulders shook and her knees started to buckle.

"Claire?" Matt said, rushing over to her. "Hey, what's wrong?"

"I just love Dempsey so much. But this applicant… she sounds so perfect and just right for Dempsey. I know this woman will appreciate her as much as I do. I can feel it just by having read the application." Fresh sobs racked her entire body.

Matt pulled her into his arms. "Oh, honey. It's hard to let go. I know."

He didn't know. He didn't.

"I don't want to give her up. I love that dog, dammit."

"I know you do. Could you keep her?"

She felt herself go limp against Matt, grateful he was holding her. But then she remembered where she was, who was keeping her upright, and she sucked in a breath and stepped back, swiping at her eyes. "I go through this with every dog. I love them so hard, and it's my job to prepare them for their furever home. It's what a foster parent signs up for. I know there are 'foster fails' out there, those who do keep their dogs, but I feel like that would be wrong. I'm meant to take in dogs who can't find homes and work with them until they're so ready, they're irresistible. And now Dempsey is."

"She is pretty irresistible," he said, going over to Dempsey and petting her.

"You knocked for dog bags and got a crying Claire. Sorry you asked, huh?" She walked back to the kitchen, pulled two poop bags from the doggie-drawer and handed them to him.

"Never," he said, stuffing the bags in his pocket. "I'm here for you. You can always talk to me."

"Till the end of March, anyway."

He winced slightly. "I guess the key is not to love the dogs when you have to give them away. I mean, you know you're not keeping them. It's not a permanent arrangement. So why get attached?"

She gaped at him. "How could I not?" Was he seriously asking this?

"You just don't. You know what you're walking into, and you create boundaries. That easy."

"Oh, really?" she said. "Well, it's not that easy for

most people. Just you. I don't know one foster parent who hasn't gotten choked up about bringing their dogs and cats to their forever homes. Not one. And you know what, Matt Fielding? I don't think you'll find it so easy to let Sparkle go."

"Trust me, I will."

"Having Hank won't protect you from having to say goodbye to that adorable fluffy little dog that you trained for weeks."

"Boundaries. It's all about boundaries."

"I guess you'd know!" she shouted and ran into her bedroom and closed the door.

She closed her eyes and shook her head, wondering what had happened to good ole levelheaded, even-keeled Claire Asher.

The hot dude in the living room happened.

Dempsey's application happened.

Boundaries were for toxic people in your life. Not for the good ones. Not for the furbabies, who saved you as much as you saved them. Even if you were just their temporary foster parent.

She heard the sliding glass door open and close, and she breathed a sigh of relief that he was gone. She ran back out into the hallway, and there was her beloved Dempsey, staring forlornly at Matt's back as he went to get Sparkle and Hank from the yard.

"Oh, Dempsey," she said, lowering to the floor on her knees and giving the sweet boxer mix a hug. "Your new mama sounds wonderful. She even has trails behind her house that you can explore."

Dempsey licked her face. Good thing too, because the tears came crashing down.

"I love you, Demps," she said, placing her forehead on the dog's warm neck, her body shuddering with fresh sobs. "I'm going to cry my eyes out and recommend the application back to Birdie. Then when it's time to bring you to your new home, I'll cry some more and foster a new pooch, and the cycle will start all over again. Because that's what it's all about.

"I might be heartbroken to lose you, but at least I feel something."

Chapter Ten

"Where should I put this, Birdie?" Matt asked, picking up the huge fifty-pound bag of dog food that some-one had donated to the shelter.

After what had just happened with Claire, he'd needed to get out of the house and, at the same time, feel connected to her, to what she was going through. He hadn't wanted to think too deeply about why. So he'd grabbed his phone and called the shelter, and Birdie happened to answer. He'd asked if she could use an extra pair of hands at Furever Paws right now, and she'd said *always*, so he'd driven over.

"We have a storage closet in the back hallway," Birdie said. "I'll show you. How's our Hank doing?"

Matt smiled. "He's doing great. He keeps that little spitfire Sparkle in line, that's for sure."

Bunny came out of the cat adoption room and smiled at Matt. "I miss his sweet face. But I sure am glad he's with you now."

He pictured Sparkle and Hank, who were probably curled up in the huge memory foam dog bed, Sparkle in her preferred napping position, with her head tucked between her front paws. *Would* he have trouble giving Sparkle up? He had a feeling he would if didn't have Hank. And if he didn't have Hank, he'd have to go get himself a Hank. So why didn't Claire have a dog of her own? Suddenly, it struck him as strange. He'd have to ask her the next time he saw her—if she was speaking to him.

"Oh, Bunny," Birdie said, turning to her sister as she stopped in front of the storage closet. "I meant to tell you—Gator texted earlier."

Birdie, Bunny and Gator. Their other brother, Moose, had passed away years ago. Since he'd started volunteering at Furever Paws, Matt had heard the Whitaker sisters talk about their family quite a bit. Birdie held Gator in high regard, and as the no-nonsense woman didn't suffer fools, he figured Gator had to be something special.

He'd learned, from overhearing many conversations between the sisters, that the Whitaker siblings had inherited the Whitaker Acres land from their parents, who'd lived in Spring Forest for generations. Gator and Moose had sold their shares long ago, but the sisters had hung on to forty acres, smartly selling small sections of their property and living off their investments.

Bunny smiled. "Oh, how nice. And what did our brother have to say for himself?"

Birdie bit her lip, something Matt didn't think he'd ever seen her do. Bernadette "Birdie" Whitaker could wrestle a crocodile, so when she seemed off balance, Matt noticed. "Well, he thinks we should sell off a parcel of the property, namely the large acreage we use as an outside dog run and training area."

Bunny frowned. "Really? Well, I don't know about that, Birdie. That would leave the shelter with little room for outdoor areas—especially if we expand in years to come."

"I know," Birdie said with a bit of a shrug. "But that was his recommendation."

As always, Matt tried not to eavesdrop but since the Whitaker sisters were talking right in front of him, he couldn't help but listen.

"Gator's never let us down with his investment recommendations," Birdie added, "but I'll talk to him about selling a parcel on the far side of the shelter instead."

"I thought the two of you owned the land outright," Matt said, looking from Birdie to Bunny. "Why would it be Gator's decision? If you don't mind my asking."

During one of their talks about Furever Paws, Claire had mentioned that most of the Whitaker land was undeveloped forest with some creek-front areas. But apparently the region was in the midst of a development boom, and the sisters had been getting offers to buy them out for years, especially by the neighboring Kingdom Creek housing development, where Matt now lived in Claire's house. According to Claire, the sisters had refused all offers; they intended to leave Whitaker Acres as a trust. Now, the Kingdom Creek development wanted to buy land right on top of the shelter. Gator seemed to think that was a good thing.

"Oh, we like to keep our attention on the furbabies and the running of the rescue, not on the business and financial end," Birdie explained. "That's Gator's specialty, and he's proven time and again he's a shrewd financial planner."

He nodded and put away the giant bag of dog food in the closet and shut the door. The rescue, surrounding area and the sisters' farmhouse were all in great condition, so it looked like the way the sisters had chosen to operate Furever Paws was working just fine. Besides, they had been living off their investments for years, so Gator Whitaker had to know what he was doing.

Matt envied what the sisters had built here. They had such rich, full lives, worked at something they loved and were so passionate about, gave back to the community over and over, and lived on their own terms. He admired the Whitaker sisters. They might not think of themselves as businesswomen, but they most definitely were.

"Bunny! Birdie!" a woman called out from the direction of the lobby. "Someone just dumped two dogs from a car and sped off!"

What the hell? Matt glanced at Birdie's and Bunny's concerned faces and followed the women as they rushed out to the lobby. Lisa Tish, one of the volunteers at Furever Paws, stood frowning in front of the door.

The young woman looked to be on the verge of tears. "I was manning the front desk when I saw the car stop up the road. A man got out and practically dragged both dogs from the car, then sped off. I saw the dogs run after the car, and then they ran back to the exact spot he'd left them. They're just sitting there!"

Matt's mouth dropped open. "He dumped them? What the hell?"

"Unfortunately, it happens all the time," Bunny said, grabbing two long rope-style leashes from the counter.

Birdie nodded and let out a deep sigh. "Twice last week." She took a handful of soft treats from the jar on the desk, put them in her pocket, and they all headed out.

Matt could see the two medium-sized dogs, one black and tan, the other mostly brown, standing up the road. That area could get busy, and he hoped the dogs would stay put until the sisters could get to them.

"Hey, pups," Bunny called in a warm, friendly voice. "Got some treats for you."

The two dogs, who looked like hound mixes, stared at Bunny. The mostly-brown one had floppy ears and seemed to have some beagle in him. The black-and-tan dog was possibly a coonhound mix, Matt thought. Two weeks ago he couldn't have told anyone the difference between a hound and a shepherd, and suddenly he could pick out breeds in a mutt.

"These treats are yummy peanut butter," Bunny added, slowly walking a bit farther as the rest of them hung back.

Matt wondered if the dogs would take off scared the

way that little gray dog had, or if they'd come running for the treats.

They came slowly toward her for the treats. Relief flooded him. He had no idea why he cared so much about two dogs that he'd never seen before two seconds ago, but hell, he did.

The sisters gave the dogs a once-over. "No collars," Bunny said, "but they do look to be in decent shape. Maybe old hunting dogs that stopped doing their 'jobs.'"

"I'd love to get my hands on that jerk," Matt said, shaking his head. "They weren't useful so he just abandoned them?"

"Like I said, it happens a lot," Bunny said. "I'm just glad folks know we're here and at least abandon them on our property." She turned to Lisa. "I'm glad you saw it happen and called us right away. Otherwise, they might have run off along the road."

Lisa nodded. "I'm with Matt. I just can't believe someone would do this. Dump dogs like that." She shook her head.

Birdie slipped a leash over the larger dog's head. The rope-like leash worked as a collar and lead in one. "Well, that's what we're here for, so all's well that ends well, right, handsome one?" she cooed to the hound. "What a majestic-looking hound you are," she said, patting his side. "Good dog. You look like a Captain to me."

Bunny put the leash over the other dog's head and secured it. She gave him a pat too. "And I'd say you look like a Major."

Matt smiled. "No Corporal?"

"Doesn't roll off the tongue as easily," Birdie said. "But the next cat that comes in will be named Corporal in honor of your service, Matt."

He laughed. "I wasn't fishing."

"Well, you've done so much for us in such a short time that you deserve it," Birdie told him.

He smiled, his chest tightening. How had he made all these connections in Spring Forest? He hadn't intended to. Was Claire right about him accidentally making a life for himself here?

"We sure owe Claire for bringing you into our lives," Bunny added as they started back toward the shelter building.

Matt frowned.

"Now, Bunny, Matt came here on his own, remember? He didn't even know Claire volunteered here when he came to look for a puppy for his niece."

Bunny seemed to think about that for a moment. "Oh, yeah."

"I guess I just associate you two with each other. Matt and Claire. Claire and Matt."

Had the temperature suddenly increased? It was barely fifty degrees today, and Matt felt feverish. There was no Matt and Claire.

Birdie smiled and patted his hand. "Why don't you go up ahead and ready two kennels while I call Doc J and let him know we have two new dogs for assessment?"

"Will do," he said, taking both leashes and bringing the dogs inside the shelter and down the hallway into the Dogs room.

"Hey, Tucker," he said as he passed the chiweenie's kennel. "Some new friends for you to sniff from afar."

Tucker ignored him, as usual, but Matt threw him a treat. The little guy ambled over for it. Someone was going to snap him up soon, Matt had no doubt.

Lisa opened the kennels for Matt, and he ushered each dog inside. "I wish I could take them both in myself, even as a foster mom," she said to Matt. "I used to have dogs, two that I adopted from here long ago, but now that I have young children and one is allergic, I have to get my fix by volunteering here when my kids are in preschool."

Matt smiled. "I get it. Before I started volunteering here, I had no idea just how much I loved dogs. Now, I can't imagine ever not having one. Or two."

She laughed. "Yup."

The door opened and Claire came in, saw him and frowned, then turned right back around.

How had things gotten so bad between them?

Because of you, idiot. Push, pull. Pull, push. You tell her no, then you're naked in bed together. And you wonder why she hates your guts.

Except she didn't hate him. And he was *hurting* her.

He felt like crud. Now he was making Furever Paws awkward and uncomfortable for her by just being here. This was *her* place, her sanctuary. And he was ruining it for her.

He loved it here too, and had only another few weeks to help out. Hell, maybe he should move out of her house. He probably should. But he couldn't go back to Laura's since Sparkle wasn't 100 percent ready. So where could he go?

His phone rang—an unfamiliar number. "Hello?"

"Matt, this is Jessica Panetta, Ellie's teacher at Spring Forest Elementary."

His heart stopped. "Is everything okay? Is Ellie okay?"

"Oh, yes! I'm sorry, I should have opened with that, the way the school's nurse does when she calls parents. Ellie is just fine. I'm calling because after I met you and Sparkle in the park a few weeks ago, I couldn't stop thinking about how wonderful it would be to have a show-and-tell about puppies and what goes into training them. Kids beg their parents for puppies, but they really don't know the work that goes into training a puppy and taking care of one. I've spoken to the principal, and she agrees it would be a great experience for the kids."

"Wait, you want me to come in and give a talk on training puppies?" he asked, completely dumbfounded.

"Exactly. I envision you bringing in Sparkle and giving a twenty-minute presentation on puppy training and what goes into it. If you like the idea, our principal only requests that you have someone from Furever Paws accompany you as a second pair of eyes and hands."

Oh God. Was this conversation actually happening? She had to be kidding.

"I just saw how good you were with that dog," the teacher continued, "the way she listened to you, how much work you clearly were putting into the training, and I knew it would be a truly special extra learning event for the kids. And to be honest, I think Ellie would enjoy a little spotlight."

His heart dropped. He remembered Ellie saying she didn't have a best friend when they first met Sparkle. Did she have friends at all?

If twenty minutes of his time would make a difference for Ellie at school, that was all he needed to know.

"I'm in," he said. "And I'm sure someone from the shelter will be happy to help me out for the presentation."

"Great!" Mrs. Panetta said. They set a date and time for the week after next, and when Matt clicked End Call, he actually had to sit down for a second.

Matt Fielding, talking to a classroom full of kids? About puppies and training them?

His life was sure taking crazy routes.

Someone from Furever Paws to be an extra set of eyes and hands... He could ask Birdie or Bunny, but Claire was a teacher and she'd be able to give him pointers on how to set up the presentation. Then again, she probably couldn't just leave her own school to help out at the elementary school, even for just twenty minutes or so.

He could ask. Because it would give him a meaningful reason to spend some time with her despite everything in him telling him to keep his distance. And no matter how he tried, he just couldn't keep away from her.

A couple of hours later, as Hank and Sparkle ran around in the enclosed dog run at the park, Matt sat on the bench near the fence with his phone, reading through the online classifieds from the free weekly newspaper's website, circling possibilities for rooms for rent. Ever since seeing Claire at Furever Paws earlier, the look on her face, the hurt and confusion and sorrow in her eyes—caused by him—he knew that moving out of the apartment at Claire's was the right thing to do. To give them both space, to keep them from constantly running into each other in the yard. This way, if she did want to work with him on the school presentation, she wouldn't be overloaded with his presence.

He read through the ads. There was a boardinghouse, and he could always move in there temporarily. Or even an inn or motel, but then again, they wouldn't allow two dogs.

All he knew for sure was that he had to let Claire be.

"Hey, Fielding!"

Matt turned around and smiled. His old neighbor, Zeke Harper, was jogging toward him. Several years younger than Matt, and tall and strong in his running gear, Zeke reminded Matt of how much he used to love to run. Maybe one of these days.

"Hey, Matt, how's the pup training going?" Zeke asked, pulling the wireless ear pods out and putting them in his pocket.

"So good, in fact, that I adopted a dog of my own," Matt said, pointing at Hank beyond the fence. The three-legged old guy was doing great keeping up with the younger pups.

Zeke grinned. "That's great! And I hear that PT I

recommended is working out too." He watched the dogs run. "You're really settling in, Matt. Glad to see it."

"Hardly settling in," Matt said. "In fact, the opposite. I'm in need of place to live."

"Didn't you say you were renting Claire Asher's apartment in Kingdom Creek?"

The sound of her name brought her face to mind. Beautiful Claire with the kind, intelligent green eyes and all that silky blond hair. "Yeah, but maybe it's better that we're not that close, you know?"

Zeke nodded. "Understood. A friend of mine has a small, furnished carriage house available right now. Not too far from my place. It's month-to-month, so since you're planning on leaving town, that might work out. And he has a dog himself, so I'm sure pets are welcome."

"Sounds perfect." He put the contact info in his phone. That was a call he'd be making very soon.

For the next fifteen minutes, he and Zeke caught up, Matt explaining that he now volunteered at Furever Paws and spent a lot of time studying up on dog training and dog psychology so that he could be even more helpful to Birdie and Bunny and the least adoptable dogs at the shelter. He felt a real kinship with those who were always left behind.

"That's really something," Zeke said. "You know I'm a psychologist and volunteer with Veterans Affairs, and I have to say I'm really intrigued by what fostering and training Sparkle and adopting Hank has done for you."

"What do you mean?"

"Well, last time I ran into you, you were saying your

life was up in the air and you felt off balance because of it. Sounds to me like volunteering at the shelter, training the puppy for your niece and adopting a dog for yourself have given you purpose. And more too—a real sense of meaning. We already know how much comfort dogs give, but the purpose side of things—that's something I'd like to bring up to my colleagues over at VA."

Huh. Matt had to admit it was all true. His life *did* have meaning now. Purpose. When the hell had all that happened? And there was something else too. Something that had shocked him when he first noticed it. "I'll be the first to say that I went from having a nightmare a night to hardly any, especially since I adopted Hank." He'd had no idea just how much comfort a dog could be.

"You know, Matt, there's someone I'd really like for you to meet. His name is Bobby Doyle, and he's one of the vets I work with at the center. He has an auto body business he's trying to get off the ground, and didn't you say your expertise in the military was with vehicle mechanics? I bet he'd value your input as a former soldier."

"He's all alone?" Matt asked.

"Actually, he has a devoted wife and two great kids," Zeke said. "Thanks to them—and *for* them—he's making great strides." He glanced at the dog run. "I've suggested that Bobby get a therapy dog who is trained to help vets dealing with PTSD."

Matt knew full-well what a great idea that was. "I could talk to Claire and the Whitaker sisters about that. Maybe they know of programs in the area that match dogs with vets."

"I'd appreciate that," he said. "And, in the meantime,

I'll give Bobby your contact info and let him know you'd be happy to hear from him."

They shook hands, and as Zeke took off running again, Matt thought about all the man had said. Matt had never paid much attention to purpose and meaning all that mumbo jumbo because his life had been chock-full of both during his army years. And here he was, a civilian, traces of the injury still dogging him every now and then, and he had purpose and meaning up the wazoo. To the point that he was actually asked—him, Matt Fielding—to present a puppy training show-and-tell to a bunch of third-graders.

Once again, how had all this happened without him noticing?

A rambunctious little terrier was being a pain in the butt in the dog run, so Matt wanted to get Sparkle and Hank out of there. Sparkle was a toughie who gave back what she got, but Hank was a gentle giant who'd let the bully nip his ankles, and he had only three to spare.

He quickly pulled out his phone and called the number Zeke had given him for the carriage house to rent. He made an appointment to see the apartment in an hour. He'd bring the dogs home, then head over.

As he was helping Sparkle up into his car, something occurred to him. If his life *did* have purpose and meaning, then he did have something to offer Claire Asher.

Whoosh! It was like getting a surprise left hook in the stomach.

So why was he still so set on keeping his emotional distance from her?

Chapter Eleven

"Well, Dempsey," Claire said. "This is goodb—" Tears filled her eyes, and she swiped them away. "I promised you I wouldn't cry, didn't I? And I'm a blubbering mess."

She sat in her car, Dempsey sitting shotgun in the passenger seat. The beautiful boxer mix looked lovely, all fresh from the groomer's and smelling slightly of lavender.

"We were only together seven weeks, and I feel like it's been forever, Demps," she said, her hands on either side of the dog's snout. "But your new mama? She really seems wonderful. She even asked me to meet her for coffee yesterday and tell her every detail about you so she could understand your every nuance. She wrote down your favorite food and treats, too, and your favorite places to trail walk."

The woman really seemed perfect, the best possible forever home for Dempsey.

"It's time, sweet girl," Claire said, getting out of the car.

Kelly Pfieffer came running out of the house. "Dempsey's here!" The woman was even planning to keep Dempsey's name to make things easier for the transition.

I've been through this before, and I'll go through it again, she thought, forcing herself to smile for Kelly. This was a big moment for both adoptive mom and Dempsey and she didn't want to make this about her.

She waved at Kelly and kneeled down next to Dempsey. "I love you, sweet girl. You're the best. And you're going to have a great life. And I promise we'll see each other at the dog park, okay?"

Dempsey put her paw on Claire's arm, and she almost lost it, but held it together.

Kelly raced over, fawning and fussing over Dempsey, thanking Claire profusely, and then soon enough, Claire was in her car alone.

She let herself cry for a good minute before driving right over to the shelter. Bunny sat behind the reception desk.

"I just dropped off Dempsey with her new mom," she said, tears still in her eyes. "I need a toughie. A foster dog who really needs me."

"Aww," Bunny said, coming around the desk to wrap Claire in a much-needed hug. "It's always so hard to give up the fosters. Especially when we bond with them.

But the bonding is what makes them so ready for that forever home. Right?"

Claire blinked back tears. "Right. Dempsey is special, and I know she's in a great home now. Letting her go was rough, I'll tell ya."

"I had one of those heart-wrenchers," Bunny said. "Remember Buttercup? Long-haired dachshund? I was crazy about that little gal. I almost kept her too. But then I remembered my mission—to prepare as many rescue dogs as I can for great new homes. Not to keep every one I fall madly in love with."

"It is really hard to let go of someone you're madly in love with," Claire agreed, her voice cracking.

"Oh, Claire, I'm so sorry Matt is a stubborn fool. A helpful one, but a stubborn fool when it comes to what's right in front of his face."

"Thanks, Bunny," Claire said. "So, who do you have for me? Distract me with a real needy one."

Bunny put her fingers on her chin. "Oh, have I got the pooch for you. Remember the black-and-white shepherd mix that came in two days ago? Doc J has him on medication for a bad ear infection, and he doesn't seem to know any commands. He's very timid. He's praise and food motivated, so I have no doubt you'll do wonders with him."

Blaze. For the white lightning bolt-like zigzag on his otherwise black head. "I'll go see him."

Blaze was in the far-left kennel. He was pressed up against the back of the kennel on a blanket, his head down, and looked pretty scared.

"Hey, boy," she said gently.

The dog lifted his green eyes first, then his head. She held out a treat, and he came padding over very slowly. Claire could have counted to twenty-five in the time it took him to reach the front of the kennel.

"Hi, Blaze," she said, giving him the treat through the bars. "Aren't you handsome? It's no fun to be in here, is it?"

The dog stared at her, and she could swear he was saying, *Please pick me to be your new foster dog. I need you, Claire.*

When she opened the kennel, he ran toward the back, flattening himself against the far side. "It's okay, Blaze. I'm all about love and treats."

"She's telling you the truth," a familiar voice said.

She whirled around to find Matt returning Tucker to his kennel and latching the door.

"I've been walking all the dogs," he said. "I even walked Blaze about an hour ago. Shy guy."

"I'm hoping to bring him out of his shell," she said, turning her attention to the dog as she leashed him and led him out of the kennel. His ears were back, which meant he was scared. "It's okay, Blaze," she said softy as she knelt down beside him. "You're coming home with me, sweetie pie. And I'm going to give you a ton of TLC as I get you ready for your forever home."

"Are *you* okay?" Matt asked as she stood up, and she was touched that he remembered today was the day she had to say goodbye to Dempsey. But of course he remembered and asked how she was doing—because he was Matt Fielding and a great guy, dammit.

She glanced at him and nodded, blinking back the

sting of tears that poked at her eyes. "It's never easy to say goodbye. But I'll tell you, it feels good to say hello. This sweetie already has my heart."

He smiled and shook his head. "I don't know how you do it. But I'm glad you do."

His tone was so reverent that she looked at him, and all she wanted to do was fling herself in his arms and be held. It would be a while before Blaze became a cuddler, if he ever did. And Claire could use some cuddling.

"I have a big favor to ask," he said.

"If I can, I will." She *could* start changing that motto. And just say no.

"Ellie's teacher called me and asked if I'd bring in Sparkle for a presentation on how to train and care for puppies. She thought it would give Ellie a little boost in the class too, which is why I couldn't say no, even though I have no idea how to present anything, let alone to kids."

"You're great with one third-grader in particular," she pointed out. "The class will love you. Plus, Sparkle will do most of the work for you by being adorable and keeping the kids' attention."

"I'm hoping so. But here's the thing. The principal says someone from Furever Paws has to be present as an extra pair of ears and eyes, just in case. I know your hours are probably the same as the elementary school's, though. We'd go on at two thirty."

She remembered Bunny's advice—not to run and hide from him. The more time they spent together— quality time—the more he might see that they belonged together. Unless she was kidding herself. "Actually, I monitor a study hall as my last period of the day. I can easily have someone cover that for me."

"Perfect. And you'll help me figure out what to say? How to structure the twenty minutes?"

"I'd love to. Dogs and kids are my two favorite things." *Add in being with you, and it's heaven.*

He smiled, but then the smile faded. Uh-oh. "Look, I know things between us have been strained and the push-pull is my fault. So, I thought it best if I find a new place to live for the next few weeks."

She didn't want him to go. Closer was better, as much as it hurt. "Matt, you don't have to do that."

"I already did."

It probably was for the best, but it still stung. Like everything these days. She shrugged. "Okay."

"Okay."

Except it wasn't okay. He was running away before he even ran away for good. This time, across town, probably near where he grew up.

"I'll miss Sparkle and Hank," she said, hoping her voice wouldn't crack.

And I'll miss you.

"I owe you a lot, Claire," he said.

"Well," she started, but what could she say? What was there to say at this point?

You need to replace Matt Fielding the way you have to replace Dempsey, her sister had texted earlier, when Claire said her heart was in pieces. New foster dog to dote on—new man to fall for.

Or maybe Claire should just focus on the dog. And the child she wanted. There were some options she could look into. Becoming a foster parent to a little kid. Foreign adoption. The ole sperm bank. She'd always wanted the traditional setup—spouse, at least two kids and dogs—but that wasn't what life had set out for her.

"I'd better get Blaze home before he thinks he's going back in the kennel," she said. "He seems almost excited."

"His tail is giving a little wag," Matt agreed.

"Guess I might not even see you leave the apartment," she said, "since all you have is a duffel bag. No moving van." She was rambling, she realized, and clamped her mouth closed.

"Don't forget the two dogs," he said with a killer smile. "Or the fact that I'd never leave without saying goodbye, Claire. I'll text you about getting together to work on the presentation."

She managed something of a smile, and watched him walk away and disappear through the door into the hallway.

"It's you and me, Blaze." The scared dog looked up at her, holding eye contact. She almost gasped, and gave the pooch a peanut butter treat. "Good dog!" she said, with a pat on his back. "And good sign."

For Blaze. And Claire's entire life.

Two weeks later, Matt looked at Sparkle, sitting very nicely after the *stay* command he'd issued, and declared her done. Her favorite treat, a chicken-flavored soft chew, was fifteen feet in front of her, and though she wanted it, she'd obeyed Matt's command and had for the past three days. She was fully trained. She knew *sit, stay, come, heel* and *drop it*, and a few others that Matt had taught her. Occasionally, she chased her tail, but now it was just cute.

He wanted to call Claire and tell her, to have her come give Sparkle the "Claire Asher, dog whisperer" stamp of approval, but since he'd moved out of her apartment and into the carriage house, he'd avoided her except to get together to structure the presentation to Ellie's class. He volunteered at Furever Paws only on days when she wasn't due in. He missed the hell out of her, but it was for the best, for both their sakes.

The doorbell rang and he answered the door, his niece Ellie flinging himself at him and wrapping her skinny arms around him.

"You're the best uncle in the world!" she said. "Thank you a million zillion times for training Sparkle!" She raced over to the puppy. "Come, Sparkle," she said very seriously.

The puppy padded over, wagging her tail.

"Good, Sparkle!" Ellie said, dropping down to her knees and petting the dog all over. "She is going to make everyone in my class wish they could have a puppy!"

No doubt. Or maybe not. "Well, tomorrow afternoon, when everyone sees how much work went into training her, how much picking up poop is involved…"

It *had* been a lot of work. And he'd loved just about every minute of it, despite the middle-of-the-night potty breaks in the freezing cold. And thanks to the presentation scheduled for tomorrow, he'd been able to get together with Claire twice over the past week. She'd kept the sessions short, making excuses to get home to Blaze, but he couldn't blame her for wanting to keep her distance.

Ellie laughed. "I don't mind picking up gross poop because that's what taking care of Sparkle is all about."

He held up his hand for a high five. "Exactly. So I'll see you at your school at two thirty."

Ellie beamed. "Yay! I'm so excited! Everyone will get to meet my great puppy!"

"Thank you, Matt," his sister said. "For *everything*. Come over anytime to visit Sparkle."

Ellie clipped on Sparkle's leash and headed toward the door. She turned to the dog. "I can't wait to show you my room."

A minute later they were gone, and it was just him and ole Hank. Matt dropped down on the couch, the big dog slowly sinking down on the rug, his head on his paws. "You're relieved that little pest is gone, aren't you?" Matt asked, laughing. Hank lifted his head. "No? You're not. Hell, I'm not either. I loved that little mutt."

The place seemed so empty without Sparkle. Even with Hank there. As the day wore on, he felt the puppy's absence so acutely that he wanted to talk about it with Claire. She'd understand exactly how he felt.

And he owed her an apology for the "you can't get attached" crud he'd tried to feed her. He'd gotten attached to Sparkle. He *was* attached to Hank.

Luckily, he couldn't go see Claire even though he thought it was a good idea. He had a job interview. His old friend Zeke had hooked him up with the veteran he'd told Matt about at the dog park. Bobby Doyle owned an auto body shop and needed some help—temporary was fine—because his best mechanic was out with a back injury. Matt quickly understood what Zeke hadn't said—that Bobby, who suffered from PTSD, could use a steadying presence like Matt around, a guy who'd been injured in a blast overseas and had come back and was piecing his life together. Bobby had built a good life for himself, but despite the family and the business, the man had trouble seeing what was right in front of him. The nightmares made it worse too. Matt had spoken to Birdie about hooking Bobby up with a program that matched therapy dogs with veterans, and Birdie was working on it.

Once Bobby's mechanic returned to work at the end of March, Matt would be leaving Spring Forest. A week, maybe ten days at most. He and Hank would hit the road and settle somewhere and start over. Matt was sure now he'd find work as a mechanic, and lately, he was thinking he might go to dog training school and become certified to work in an animal shelter, maybe even start his own business.

His life was moving forward in the right direction. He wasn't there yet, but maybe he'd get there. Then maybe there could be a chance for him and Claire.

Whoa. He'd had that thought and had always pushed it back down in the recesses where it belonged. But now it was up and out there. He could no longer deny that things were happening for him, that he was building something here in Spring Forest without ever having meant to.

Which meant he'd actually stay?

He looked at Hank. "What the hell, buddy? Why don't I know what's up from one minute to the next? Why is this so damned hard?"

Hank came over and put his head on Matt's thigh. He could swear the dog was saying, "I know, right?"

Eighteen third-graders, including his niece, Ellie, were staring at him as he stood at the blackboard in the front of the classroom, Sparkle on a four-foot leash beside him in the *sit* position. Mrs. Panetta's desk was to his left, and Claire stood just slightly behind him on his right, next to Sparkle's kennel. He'd walked the dog in on her leash, and the moment they'd entered the classroom, the kids had gone crazy with oohs and aahs, so cute, aww, throwing out tons of questions about how much she weighed and how old she was and if she knew she was a dog. Mrs. Panetta had gotten them to shush and explained that Mr. Fielding—man, did that sound weird—would answer all their questions after his presentation.

Ellie sat in the first row, just to the left of him. Next to her was a girl with her arms folded over her chest, who seemed to be sulking. Maybe her parents wouldn't let her have a dog. The boy on the other side of the sulker was grinning like crazy, and could barely contain his excitement about having a puppy in his classroom.

The teacher had introduced him and Claire, so he'd better get cracking.

"Hi, kids," he began. "About a month ago, my niece Ellie was promised a puppy for her birthday, which is coming up in just a few days. So I took Ellie to the

Furever Paws shelter to pick one out. Who did she fall in love with? A totally untrained five-month-old puppy that wouldn't stop barking or spinning in circles and chasing her tail, and had no idea that she wasn't supposed to go potty in the house."

The kids broke into laughter at that one. Ellie was beaming, and Matt winked at her.

"Well, my sister, Ellie's mom, wanted a trained puppy," he continued. "So I offered to turn Sparkle into just the right puppy for their house. It was a lot of hard work. Sparkle had to learn her name, to come when called, to stay when told to stay, not to chase birds or squirrels when told no, not to jump up and—very importantly—to do her business, if you know what I mean, outside only."

"You mean pee and poop!" the excited boy shouted.

"Exactly," Matt said, laughing.

He handed Sparkle's leash to Claire, then moved to the far end of the classroom. "Sparkle!"

The dog immediately looked at him.

"Sparkle, come!" She came trotting over, Claire more holding the leash than guiding her. He led her back to the front of the room, then put a treat down on the floor right in front of Sparkle. "Now, this is Sparkle's favorite treat. Peanut butter. Oh boy, does she love peanut butter."

The sulking girl in the front shot her hand in the air.

"Yes, Danica?" Mrs. Panetta said.

"If it's her favorite, why isn't she eating it?" the girl demanded, crossing her arms over her chest again.

"Because I didn't tell her she could," Matt explained. "Okay, Sparkle. Treat."

The dog looked at Matt and then gobbled it up.

Everyone clapped. "Ellie, your dog is so awesome!" someone called out.

Ellie was glowing.

"Sparkle, treat!" Danica said, holding out what looked like half of a chocolate bar.

"No, Sparkle!" Claire shouted. "Stay! Chocolate is toxic to dogs."

"Here, Sparkle!" Danica said, waving the chocolate.

As if in slow motion, Mrs. Panetta, Matt and Claire all rushed forward—the teacher to grab the chocolate before the dog could, and Matt and Claire to get ahold of Sparkle on her leash. But the puppy lunged, jumping up on the girl and knocking her lunch box all over the floor. Her sandwich went spinning—and Sparkle went flying after it.

"Sparkle, stay!" Matt commanded. The puppy stopped and looked at Matt. He scooped her up and put her in her kennel.

"Your puppy is so dumb!" Danica shouted, collecting her baggie-wrapped sandwich and putting it back in her lunch box.

"*You're* dumb!" Ellie shouted.

Oh no. Tell me this is not happening, Matt thought, his stomach sinking.

"Danica and Ellie, you're both going to the principal's office after the presentation," Mrs. Panetta said, directing a stern look at both girls.

Ellie had tears in her eyes. Danica looked spitting mad.

Great. The spotlight sure was on Ellie.

He'd blown this. He'd gotten smug, thinking he knew

everything about puppies and training, when he'd forgotten about how unpredictable things could get.

And Claire had reminded him when they'd last gotten together.

"Sparkle will be in an unfamiliar environment," Claire had said. "Lots of little hands will be poking at her, wanting to touch her. We'll have to be on guard and mindful that it may stress her, even though she's well trained."

He'd let Sparkle get too close to Danica, and now both girls were in trouble.

"Mrs. Panetta?" a boy asked, his hand in the air.

"Yes, Tom?"

"I wanted a puppy for my birthday, but now I don't," he said.

"Yeah, what if I got a puppy and it ate my Halloween candy and got sick?" a girl asked.

Sigh.

"That's a great question," Claire said, stepping forward. "And that's part of caring for a puppy. We always have to be really careful about what a dog can get ahold of. It's almost like babyproofing your house. Dogs can chew wires, they can eat things that are bad for them. Having a pet really does take a lot of work, but you know what?"

"What?" a few kids asked.

"Having a pet is also really great. You have an instant buddy, a friend to love and care for, and the rewards are worth all the hard stuff about having a pet."

"I have a dog and he's my best friend," a boy in the back said. "He sleeps next to my bed every night."

"My cat does that," another boy said.

"I hope my parents let me get a dog for my birthday. You're so lucky, Ellie," another girl said.

"Your dog is an idiot!" Danica hiss-whispered to Ellie.

"No, *you're* the idiot!" Ellie hiss-whispered back.

"Girls, that is enough," Mrs. Panetta said sharply. "Well, kids, that's it for today. Let's all thank Mr. Fielding and Ms. Asher from Furever Paws Animal Rescue for coming in today and telling us all about puppy care and training."

After lots of thank-yous, Matt picked up Sparkle's kennel and gave Ellie a quick hand-squeeze, then got the hell out of that classroom. The teacher followed him and Claire into the hallway.

"Please don't worry about things getting a bit out of hand," Mrs. Panetta said. "Claire will tell you—as a teacher, you just never know. But the presentation was great, and I think the kids got a lot out of it. Thank you so much for coming in."

Matt managed a smile and shook her hand. He needed air. Cold March air. Gripping Sparkle's kennel, he headed for the exit.

"Well, it was realistic," Claire said. "And Mrs. Panetta is right. You just never know what will happen. I hope you're not upset about the end."

He gaped at her. "Not upset? Are you kidding? This was Ellie's chance to shine. Instead, some girl tried to poison her dog, and now Ellie's in trouble for calling her dumb."

They reached the door and Claire pushed it open,

holding it for Matt who held the heavy kennel. "It happens, Matt. In third grade and in middle school and in high school. All part of learning to get along."

The cool air felt good on his heated skin, but his heart kept pounding with how badly it had all gone down. "I'd hardly call that getting along. Ellie is going to be really pissed at me, and rightly so. I didn't handle things right. Why the hell I did think I belonged in this environment? With kids and puppies? I knew better than that. But I let myself be talked into thinking I'm someone I'm not."

"Oh, Matt, come on," she said, glaring at him.

"I'm not Uncle Matt the puppy trainer, who can lead a classroom presentation," he snapped. "I'm a former army corporal with a slight limp trying to figure things out now that I'm a civilian."

"And you are," she said, touching his arm.

He pulled away. "I thought I was. But I don't belong here, Claire. This is your world. Not mine."

One thing was for damned sure. He *wasn't* staying in Spring Forest. Come the end of the month, he and his Mustang would be gone, Hank riding shotgun.

Chapter Twelve

"Claire, you know I'm not one to pry, but are you planning to get pregnant by a sperm donor?"

Claire almost spit out the sip of water she'd just taken. She straightened the stack of applications for tomorrow's adoption event and moved them to the counter. How on earth would Bunny know she was looking into options? Then she eyed her tote bag, which had slumped over on the desk. The big pamphlet for "Is Using a Sperm Donor Right for You?" was sticking out.

She sighed. A week had passed since the fiasco in Ellie's class. A week without a word from Matt, despite her texting and calling and even showing up at his place and knocking on the door. She'd peered in the windows, and he didn't seem to be home, so maybe he wasn't avoiding her. She'd heard Hank's nails scrape the floor as he'd come to the door to see who was there, and she'd been almost doubled-over with pangs of missing the old dog. Missing Matt.

She glanced around the lobby. The two of them were alone, thank goodness. Claire shoved the pamphlet back in the bag and hung it on the back of the chair. "Just looking into all possibilities," she whispered.

"I understand," Bunny said. "Believe me."

Claire was about to use the opportunity to ask Bunny about her personal life. She knew Bunny had been engaged in her twenties and that her fiancé had died tragically. Bunny often mentioned the man with a sweet, wistful tone, and Claire had always wanted to know Bunny's story—how he'd died, if Bunny had tried to find love after her loss.

But before Claire could think of a nonprying way to pry, Bunny rushed to say, "Guess things aren't working out with Matt?"

Sometimes Claire wasn't sure if Bunny wanted to be asked about her life or not. Her money was on the latter. "Nope. I tried everything, Bunny. But the man insists, once again, that he's not future material, no one's husband or father, and is planning to leave town at the end of the month. And March is almost over, so…probably Sunday night."

"Stubborn fool," Bunny said, shaking her head.

Claire couldn't help but smile. "Thanks."

Birdie came in from the back hallway, carrying a donation of stacked empty litter boxes, and Claire jumped up to take them from her. "Thanks, Claire. Would you mind logging these in?"

Claire was glad to be busy. She'd walked all the dogs, played with them individually and together in the yard, swept, sanitized, and now she was looking for things to do to avoid thinking about Matt. In fifteen minutes she'd be done here, and would go home to sweet Blaze. The noon dog walker reported that Blaze was a bit skittish on leash when other dogs were nearby, and that was something Claire was working on. She adored Blaze, but Blaze wasn't a cuddler yet. He might never be, and that was okay too.

"Oh, Bunny—Gator texted about selling that parcel of land again," Birdie said.

"I don't think we should, Birdie. It's prime Furever Paws acreage!"

Birdie shrugged. "Gator said he looked deeply into it."

Claire had begun to realize that Bernadette "Birdie" Whitaker had one weakness: her brother, Gator. Bunny, who tended to defer to Birdie in most things, also had one weakness: the animals. So when there was discord about something related to Whitaker Acres, Birdie and Bunny butted heads, which was a good thing. No quick agreements on what should be carefully considered— like selling the land currently used for training the dogs.

"Tell him we're thinking about possibilities," Bunny said, giving Claire a wink.

Claire blushed. She hoped Bunny wouldn't tell Birdie that she was checking out options for having a family. Ones that didn't include a husband. She wasn't quite ready to share that yet.

Because she also wasn't ready to give up on her dreams of a future with Matt Fielding.

The bell over the front door jangled and Richard Jackson, aka Doc J, walked in. The veterinarian, a tall, kind man in his sixties, had a thriving private practice but spent a lot of time at the shelter, offering his services out of the goodness of his heart. If Claire wasn't mistaken, he'd been in more than usual the past few days, fussing over the Whitaker sisters, complimenting their hair and outfits. Considering Birdie often wore paw-muddied overalls, and Bunny liked her Crocs with animal-print socks, Claire thought it was sweet.

"I like your rabbit pin, Bunny," Doc J said with a warm smile.

"Oh, thank you," she said, peering at it on her big blue fisherman sweater. "Birdie gave it to me for my birthday. A bunny for Bunny, she said." Bunny laughed.

"And I just happen to have a bird for a Birdie and a Bunny," Doc J said, handing Birdie a bakery box.

"What's this?" Birdie asked with a surprised smile.

"Open it," Doc J said.

Birdie opened the box and placed a hand on the region of her heart. She pulled out a big cookie in the shape and colors of a robin. "A bird for a Birdie."

"There were no bunnies, or I would have gotten one," he said to Bunny. "But I did get two robins."

Bunny laughed. "You're a peach, Doc J."

Claire watched the interplay between the three and was sure the doc had a little crush on one of the sisters—she just wasn't sure which one. Hey, if Claire had

no love life, she wanted others to so she could live vi-
cariously through them.

Her phone pinged with a text. Hopefully, it wasn't
her sister with a blind date suggestion.

Nope. It was Matt.

Sparkle slipped out the front door and that moped
spooked her and she took off. Ellie's frantic. We're
searching on Holly Road. Help?

Oh God.
On my way, she texted back.
Oh no. Holly Road was busy with cars. *Please let
them find her*, she thought, rushing out the door.

"Where could she be?" Ellie asked Matt, tears
streaming down her face.

"We'll find her," he assured his niece, praying that
would be true. "Let's keep looking. Remember to use a
gentle voice if you see her and hold out the cheese stick.
Sparkle loves those."

They walked down the sidewalk, looking under cars.
No sign of the little dog.

A girl around Ellie's age stood on her lawn holding
a Hula-Hoop around her waist. As Matt got closer, he
realized it was the sulky one from Ellie's class. Luckily,
Ellie hadn't been upset at Matt for what had happened.
Instead, she'd given him an earful about how Danica
was always mean to her and that the principal had given
Danica a detention for "not being kind, and starting a
problem," whereas Ellie didn't get in trouble at all.

Ellie ran up to the girl. "Danica? Did you see a brown-and-white puppy run past your house?"

The girl barely looked at Ellie. "Yup, I did."

"Did she go that way?" Ellie asked, pointing ahead toward the intersection. It had a four-way stop sign and not a light, thank God, but it was a busy junction.

Danica nodded. "Yup. Straight into traffic and kept going. Guess your only friend is gone, Ellie," the girl said, giving the Hula-Hoop a spin. It landed on the grass, and she frowned and picked it up, giving it another spin. "Maybe she got hit by a car." She spun the Hula-Hoop again, this time working it around her narrow hips. "Too bad, so sad."

Jesus. Matt's sister often mentioned the mean-girl drama among girls of Ellie's age, and he would have sworn eight was way too young for that crud. But he'd seen it firsthand at Ellie's school, and here it was again, right in front of him.

"Danica Haverman!" A woman came around the side of the house with a gardening tool in her hand. "I heard what you said. That was very unkind."

"Her own dog doesn't like her!" Danica said, looking like she was about to cry.

Suddenly Matt realized what was going on here. The girl was very, very jealous that Ellie had a dog.

"I'd rather have no friends at all than be the meanest girl in school!" Ellie screamed.

The girl froze, and then winced and burst into tears.

"We have to go find Sparkle," Matt said to Danica's mother. "I hope they can work this out."

The woman sighed. "Me too. You go inside and

straight to your room, young lady," she added to her daughter.

Matt took Ellie's hand, and they went running down the sidewalk in the direction Sparkle had gone. They looked under every car, asked everyone they saw if he or she had seen a little brown-and-white dog. No one had.

All of a sudden, he saw Claire's car coming down Holly Road. He waved, and she parked on the street and got out. "I have mozzarella string cheese," she said, handing one each to Matt and Ellie.

"We have them too," he said, holding up the five he'd stuffed in the pocket of his leather jacket.

"What if we can't find her?" Ellie asked, her tone frantic.

"Honey," Claire said. "Sparkle has a collar with her name and your telephone number on it. Plus, she's microchipped, which means if she's turned into a shelter, they can use a scanner to read the chip and find out who she belongs to."

Matt just hoped that if they didn't find her, someone had picked her up. If that little dog got hit by a car... He was supposed to be watching Ellie for his sister, supervising her with Sparkle. This was on him.

Great job, Fielding, he thought as he got down on his hands and knees to look under a low-slung car. "Sparkle? You hiding behind those wheels?"

There was no sign of her.

"We'll find her. Or someone will," Claire said.

Matt squeezed her hand, and the moment their skin made contact, he realized how much he'd missed touching her. Missed *her*. "Thanks for coming to help."

"Hey! Are you guys looking for a missing dog?" a woman called out from across the intersection.

"Yes!" Matt shouted, and they all went running to the stop sign.

"There's a brown-and-white puppy trembling behind the wheel of this truck."

Oh thank God, Matt thought.

"Sparkle! She's alive!" Ellie exclaimed.

"Let's let Uncle Matt go get her," Claire told Ellie. "She's very used to him, and I think she'll respond best to him in this scary situation she's gotten herself into."

Ellie bit her lip. "Okay. I know you can do it, Uncle Matt."

He put his hand on Ellie's shoulder. He was not returning without that dog safe and sound in his arms. He hadn't ever been able to find the skinny gray dog they'd seen a couple of times, but he was saving Sparkle. Hell yeah, he was.

He waited for a bunch of cars to pass, then ran across the road. He got down again, wincing at the jab in his leg. There was Sparkle, on the inside of the wheel on the far side of the car. Shaking.

"Hey, girl," he said. "Silly of you to run out the door when all the good stuff is inside the house. But I do have your favorite treat. Mozzarella string cheese stick." He ripped off a chunk and held it out toward her. He wished he could grab her, but his arms would have to be ten feet long. And he wouldn't be able to reach her from the other side. Plus, he'd no doubt get hit by a car himself.

Sparkle looked at him and tilted her head, then looked at the cheese in his hand. A big SUV went by, causing her to tremble again and flatten herself against the wheel.

"Yum," he said, taking a bite for himself.

Sparkle slowly moved toward his hand, and when she went for the cheese, he put one arm around her midsection. "Good Sparkle." The dog relaxed a bit, and he gave her another bite of cheese, then he scooped her up. He braced himself against the car to stand back up. "Got her!" he called to Claire and Ellie.

His niece broke into a grin. And seeing Claire smile almost made him drop to his knees.

He attached Sparkle's leash and walked the dog over to Ellie, who smothered her in kisses.

"All's well that ends well," Claire said.

"I blew it," Matt whispered. "We got lucky, but I almost lost that dog on my watch."

"Dogs slip out, Matt. It happens."

"It shouldn't." Just another example that he didn't belong in this world of kids and dogs and people depending on him. He had no experience as Uncle Matt. He'd been winging it, and he'd had no right when a little girl's heart was at stake.

And a woman's. *Stick to your plan, Fielding*, he told himself. *You'll help out with the adoption events, then you're gone Sunday night. Someplace where you'll feel...comfortable, in the right skin*. He just had no idea where that was.

She shook her head and turned to Ellie. "I'm meeting a couple girlfriends for an early dinner, but I sure am glad I got to see you and Sparkle reunited. That's all that matters. That you're back together."

"I'm so happy. Thank you, Uncle Matt!" Ellie said, flinging herself into his arms while holding tightly on the leash.

Man, it was going to be hard to say goodbye to this sweet little girl. And as he watched Claire hug Ellie and then dash off toward her car, he knew he was going to break his own heart again by saying goodbye to her.

As he and Ellie headed back toward his sister's house, Sparkle scampering on her leash just ahead of them, Ellie stopped and said, "Uh-oh."

"What's wrong?" he asked.

"Danica Haverman's back in her yard with her dumb Hula-Hoop."

Matt glanced over. She sure was. "Well, let's see what happens."

Ellie shrugged and they resumed walking

Just as they neared Danica's yard, the girl dropped her Hula-Hoop and stared at them. She just stood there, not saying anything. Finally, she slowly came over to the end of her yard. "You found Sparkle."

Ellie tilted her head. "My uncle did. She was hiding under a car."

Danica bit her lip, looking at Ellie one second and the ground, the next. "Can I pet her?" she asked, looking sheepish. "You'll probably say no."

"I'm surprised you even want to," Ellie said, giving Sparkle a protective pat on the side.

Danica's eyes glistened with tears. "I wish I could get a dog."

Ah, Matt thought. He might not understand eight-year-old girls so well, but if he knew his niece, her next move would be kindness.

"Dogs are definitely awesome," Ellie said. "You can pet her. She's really soft."

Danica almost gasped. She bit her lip again and then both girls dropped to their knees, Danica petting Sparkle and Ellie staring at the girl in wonder.

Tears misted in Danica's eyes. "I'm sorry I said your dog didn't like you. Anyone can see she does."

"Well, I'm sorry I said you were the meanest girl in school. You're not. Because mean people don't say sorry and they don't pet puppies."

Danica beamed.

"Wanna come over later and play with her? I taught her how to fetch my socks."

Danica laughed. "Sure, I'll ask my mom."

And just like that, Ellie had a friend.

If only he and Claire could patch things up between them as easily.

Claire pulled open the door to the Main Street Grille, grateful for a little girl time. She, Amanda and fellow Furever Paws volunteer Mollie McFadden often got together for lunch or coffee after adoption events, but she was glad they'd set something up for today, just a regular ole day. Too bad her heart felt like it weighed thirty pounds.

She spotted the two young women sitting by the window. Amanda walked dogs on her day off from running the Grille, and Mollie was a dog trainer who assessed the shelter's newcomers when she had free time. Furever

Paws hadn't just brought furbabies into her life, but friends, as well.

"I hear you have a new foster!" Amanda said. "How are things going?"

Claire smiled just thinking of sweet Blaze. "So far, so good. He's on the timid side, but is slowly coming out of his shell."

"Guess who I saw in the park yesterday!" Mollie said. "Dempsey! She was with her new owner, fetching ball after ball. Oh, Claire, she looked really happy. And I heard her new owner say to her, 'you're the best dog ever, Dempsey.'"

Claire laughed, her heavy heart lightening a bit. "Good. I couldn't be happier about that match."

"I wish I could have a dog," Amanda said. "But I live here. One of these days…"

"Well, I know how much Birdie and Bunny appreciate that you come in to walk the dogs," Claire said.

Mollie leaned forward. "Speaking of shelter volunteers, my…friend Zeke is good friends with Matt. He mentioned that Matt now lives in a carriage house nearby. I thought he was living over your garage."

A waitress served the food just then, and Claire's hearty appetite for her turkey club waned. She still popped a fry into her mouth.

"Just didn't work out between us," she said, taking a bite of her sandwich to avoid having to elaborate. She couldn't talk about Matt or think about him without wanting to cry these days.

She knew he'd added the Sparkle-going-missing episode to the list of reasons why he wasn't meant to be a family man…when to her, how he'd handled it proved that he *was*.

"Sounds like you put 'friend' in air quotes, Mollie," Amanda said, adding a dollop of ketchup to her veggie burger.

They both knew that Zeke was Mollie's late brother's best friend. Zeke treated Mollie like a little sister, while she clearly had feelings for him. But she was gun-shy to act on them for fear of messing up the friendship.

Why was romance so complicated?

The door jangled and in walked Ryan Carter, the new owner and editor of the small local newspaper, the *Spring Forest Chronicle*. He headed straight to the counter, looking around for a waitress.

"Hey, Ryan," Amanda said with a warm smile and a wave. Claire knew that Amanda had developed a little crush on the newcomer. "The counter waitress is just picking up an order in the kitchen. She'll be right out."

He barely acknowledged that she'd spoken.

"Chatty, isn't he?" Mollie whispered with a devilish grin. "Gotta love the brooding types."

"What's his story?" Claire asked. "Single? Divorced?"

"No one knows," Amanda said. "He's a man of mystery, apparently."

But Claire noticed how Amanda's gaze lingered on the very attractive newsman. Yup, romance was complicated.

"Speaking of stories, what the heck is this about the crazy thunderstorm forecasted for Monday night?" Mollie asked, taking a sip of her iced tea.

Claire had just heard about the storm this morning. People were already hitting the supermarkets to stock up on water and flashlights since losing power was a strong possibility.

Dempsey never minded bad weather. But Blaze was a scaredy-dog, and she had a feeling she'd be under the covers with him during the storm.

She picked up her sandwich to take a bite when she glanced out the window and saw Matt across the street, headed into a shop, Hank's leash around the pole out front. Her heart leaped at the sight of both of them, man and dog. She missed them so much.

What she wouldn't give to be under the covers with Blaze *and* Matt when the storm struck.

Chapter Thirteen

By late Monday afternoon, all anyone could talk about was how the thunderstorm forecasted for that evening had turned into a tornado watch. If there was a tornado, it was supposed to miss Spring Forest by a good margin, but you couldn't be too careful. Matt's sister's family had left for a planned vacation to his brother-in-law's parents' place, so they and Sparkle were far from harm. He was grateful he wouldn't have to worry about them. But all *his* plans to leave Spring Forest last night had gone out the window. No way could he leave knowing the town—and the Furever Paws shelter—could be hit hard by the storm. He'd rather stay put for a day or two and just make sure the people and animals he cared about were safe. Then he'd go.

Matt had done some online research on tornado

preparation, and apparently taping windows or even cracking windows to equalize pressure was no longer considered useful. Taking down mirrors from the walls and moving other glass items under chairs, creating a safe space in the basement—preferably with no windows—and having food and water for at least seventy-two hours were all listed as steps to take.

At five o'clock he headed over to the shelter to help batten down the hatches, but when he'd arrived, Birdie and Bunny had assured him their handyman and his assistant had it covered and had handled all the storm preparation for years.

Birdie seemed to be trying her best to be strong for Bunny, even chatting about their nephew Grant, who would be visiting soon. Matt had tried "shooting the breeze" about how he remembered Grant and his sisters coming to visit and staying every summer, and how they'd all—him included—go swimming in the creek behind the sisters' farmhouse. Bunny's face had lit up with the reminiscing, and Birdie had mouthed a thank-you to him for getting her sister's mind off the impending storm, even for fifteen minutes.

His research into helping dogs through particularly severe weather had had him up all night, and this morning he'd bought a few things from the big pet emporium two towns over, including something for Blaze, which he was planning on dropping off at Claire's. He wasn't so sure she would be happy to see him, but he also wanted to make sure she had everything she needed for the storm.

He rang the bell and was greeted by a short bark.

Claire opened the door, surprise lighting her pretty face. "Hey."

"I have something for Blaze." He pulled a package from the bag. "It's a thunder shirt. It's supposed to be comforting to a dog who's afraid of thunder."

Her face softened and she knelt down in front of Blaze. "See that?" she said to the dog. "Matt got you a present to help you through tonight. That sure was kind of him." She stood up, taking the package. "Thank you."

"You probably already have one, but I just wanted to make sure."

She laughed. "I actually have three, in all sizes."

He smiled. "Well, you can never have too many thunder shirts."

"I just spoke to Bunny. They're all set over there. She and Birdie and the staff moved all the dogs and cats to the basement, and two volunteers will stay with them overnight."

"I was just over there. They said they have everything covered. But what about the barn animals?" he asked, thinking of the sweet pair of llamas that Hank liked to visit whenever they went to the shelter together. "The pigs, goats, and geese?"

"The sisters will bring the geese with them into the basement of the farmhouse for the night. They say the rest of the animals will be safe in the barn."

He sure as hell hoped so.

A crack of thunder boomed in the gray sky, and they both looked up. Blaze ran back inside under a chair in the living room.

"I might need *all four* thunder shirts for him," she said. "Thanks again, Matt."

"By the way, I put up a bunch of signs in town about the gray dog we saw—I described him best I could and asked folks to call me or Furever Paws if he's spotted or found, but I haven't had any responses. If only we'd gotten a photo, that would have helped."

She nodded. "Well, I'm sure he'll find some sort of shelter tonight. Dogs have a good sense of weather and hopefully he'll find a safe haven at the first scent of thunder."

That made him feel better in general, but he still didn't want to leave her. "Well, stay safe," he heard himself saying.

She bit her lip and grabbed him into a hug. "You too."

He froze for a moment, then pulled her tighter against him, breathing in the scent of her skin, her hair, so in need of her against him that he'd lost all ability to think.

A streak of lightning lit the sky, followed by another boom of thunder, and Claire pulled away.

"You'd better get home," she said.

I don't want to leave you, was all he could think. If he had had Hank with him, he might have found a way to invite himself in for the night, just to make sure she would be safe.

He forced himself to his car. *I don't want to leave you* echoed in his head to the point that it was louder than the rain beating against the windshield.

By seven o'clock, the rain was coming down so hard, talk of the tornado watch on the TV news freaked him out to the point that he couldn't just stay home. He had to check on the sisters, on the shelter and on the barn animals, who were all alone on Whitaker Acres. He packed up a sleeping bag, Hank's favorite bed, food and water for both of them, his phone and charger, put on his trusty L.L.Bean raincoat and muck boots and headed out.

He drove over to Furever Paws first, the concrete building strong and sturdy in the beating rain. He'd called ahead to let the two volunteers know he was coming to check on them and to see if they needed anything. They said they'd thought of everything but extra batteries for their flashlights, and asked if he happened to have any, so he brought two ten packs that he'd had in his kitchen drawer. He found them safe and sound and playing cards in the basement. Some of the dogs were howling. The tremblers who were scared of thunder were in the farmhouse with the sisters. The cats all seemed okay.

Next he drove over to the farmhouse and found Birdie and Bunny hunkered down in their basement with the special-needs dogs and cats and any ones who'd been particularly frightened in their kennels, all in thunder shirts with extra blankets to cozy up in. The geese were in a large pen.

Three booms in a row were so loud that Matt felt them in his chest. "I'm going to stay the night in the barn," he shouted above the noise. "I'll watch over the animals and be close by if you need me."

"Oh, Matt, bless you," Bunny said.

Birdie grabbed him in a hug.

He raced out to his car, his raincoat soaking wet in just seconds. He drove the one minute down the gravel road to the big barn, the windshield wipers on their fastest setting unable to keep up with the pounding rain and winds. He covered himself with a tarp and grabbed the sleeping bag and Hank's bed under it, then darted into the barn, setting up their sleeping quarters on the far side where there were no windows. The rain beat down on the roof so loud he was surprised the llamas and goats weren't trembling in their pens. The crazy thing was that the worst of the storm hadn't even started.

He went back out to the car, backing it up as close to the entrance as he could, then opened the door for Hank to jump out. He ran inside, his fur wet, and gave himself a good shake.

Matt grabbed a towel from his backpack and dried him off, giving him a pat. "You can go lie down and try to relax, buddy," he said. "It's gonna be a long night."

Another crack of thunder exploded, and Hank lifted his head from the bed. The white noise machine he'd brought to try to counteract the thunder was useless since the booms were so loud. The llamas and pigs were a noise machine in themselves; no one would be getting any sleep tonight, that was for sure.

His phone pinged with a text—from the National Weather Service. This is a weather alert. The tornado watch is now a tornado warning. The alert repeated three times.

Matt gasped. "Oh hell."

Panic gripped him as the winds began to howl. Another boom of thunder hit so loud that Matt put his arms around Hank. The senior dog didn't seem afraid of the noise, but he'd let out a low growl indicating he sure didn't like it. *Neither do I, buddy.* Grabbing his phone, he sent up a silent prayer for cell service, relief washing over him when he was able to call the Whitaker sisters. They assured him they were fine, safe in the basement with their motley crew of dogs, cats and geese, and she and Bunny were playing cards and having those robin cookies that Doc J had brought. He didn't know Birdie Whitaker all that well, but something told him she kept her fears to herself. If she needed him, he had a good feeling she'd call right away.

Another crack of thunder hit, lightning streaking across the sky. He thought of Claire, alone in the house with the timid Blaze, and tried to call her, but the screen on his phone flashed No Service. *No, no, no.* His chest got tight and his heart started beating too fast. He needed to be able to hear that she was okay. He needed to be reachable for the Whitaker sisters. *Dammit!*

He checked his phone again a few minutes later. Same thing. No Service.

He thought he heard a car door slam right outside the doors to the barn. Hank stood up, staring at the doors. "It's okay, buddy. I'll go check it out."

He unlatched the doors and threw the left side open. Claire's SUV was there, the lights shining. *What the hell?*

He ran over to the car just as she got out.

"I have to get Blaze!" she shouted over the crashing sounds of the storm. "He's in his kennel!"

"I'll get the kennel," he shouted back. "You grab your stuff."

She nodded, and he hurried to the trunk and popped it open, grabbing the kennel, which was covered with a small lined tarp.

"I've got you, Blaze. It's gonna be okay," he said in what he hoped was a soothing tone. He felt anything but soothed. He rushed the kennel inside the barn and set it down, and when Claire dashed in with her bags, he closed the barn door and latched it again.

"Claire, how could you risk it?" he asked, staring at her.

She shoved off the hood of her raincoat, her blond hair dry in a low ponytail. "I couldn't sit at home knowing the barn animals were here alone. I just couldn't."

She knelt down in front of Blaze's kennel and opened it. The dog put his snout and one paw hesitantly out onto the barn floor, then slowly came out all the way and looked around. He saw Hank over on his bed and walked over, giving a sniff, then cautiously put a paw on the bed to see how Hank would respond. Because Hank was awesome, he lay his head on the far side of the bed to make room for the smaller dog, who stepped in and curled up alongside Hank's big body.

For a moment, they both watched the dogs settle, and Matt felt more at ease, knowing the timid Blaze would be watched over by Hank tonight.

"Me too," he said. "I should have let you know I was planning to come out here. I tried to call you a minute ago, but there's no cell service."

"I'm glad you didn't reach me," she said.

"Why?" He held her gaze.

"Because I might not have come. And then I wouldn't

be with you right now. And I need to be with you right now, Matt."

He unzipped her soaked raincoat and helped her out of it, then hung it up on a peg next to his. He got his jacket off, and then, before he could stop himself, he pulled Claire into his arms. "It's going to be okay. I checked on the shelter and the sisters. Everyone's fine. Did you hear the watch has turned into a warning? And that it's supposed to strike over Spring Forest?"

She nodded, her face draining of color. "I heard on the way over. Thank God I left when I did, or I wouldn't have been able to come at all. I would have been worried sick about the barn animals here all alone." She smiled and looked at him. "I should have known you'd come."

"I should have known *you*'d come. Want me to grab anything from your car?" he asked.

"I just brought my backpack with supplies for Blaze and some water and granola bars." She clunked herself on the forehead with her palm. "Oh no, I forgot my sleeping bag at home."

"Guess we'll have to share mine," he said, pointing at the rolled-up green nylon pack near Hank's bed. "If you want," he added. "Or you could have it, and I'll make do with the extra blanket I brought. I saw a stack of blankets on a shelf too."

She glanced to where he pointed. "They're for the animals. Those blankets smell like goat and llama."

"So you'll save me from that?" he asked with a smile.

She nodded. "Thanks for offering to share your sleeping bag."

She was thanking *him*? When he'd get to spend a scary, crazy night with Claire spooned against him, safe and sound? "Blaze looks like he's doing okay," he said, his gaze on the black-and-white dog calmly lying between Hank and the wall.

Claire smiled. "I think Blaze found his safe space for tonight. Thanks, Hank."

His heart was practically bursting with how much he cared about this woman, how much he wanted her, needed her.

Over the next couple of hours, the power went out, so Matt set up a couple of flashlights to provide illumination. There was little to do but listen to the rain pound against the barn. Both of them were too wired to talk much. At around midnight, Claire slid into the sleeping bag with a yawn.

"I don't know if I'll be able to sleep," she said.

Matt slid in beside her. They were so close. To the point he could feel her body heat. "Me either."

When a crack of thunder boomed and Claire almost jumped, Matt laid a comforting, heavy hand on her shoulder and then smoothed her hair back from her face. "It's okay, everything is going to be okay." Her eyes looked heavy, as though he was lulling her to sleep, and he hoped that would be the case. Her lids fluttered closed, her breathing soft and steady, and he realized she had fallen asleep. In his arms.

He closed his eyes, his chin resting against her head. He could stay like this forever. Without the tornado, of course.

A noise unlike any Matt had ever heard raged outside, and he started, bolting upright. He'd fallen asleep too. Claire popped up, disoriented, fear in her eyes as a strange howling wind raged outside. The dogs were standing pressed against the barn wall, Blaze trying to get between his protector, Hank, and the wood.

The tornado. *Oh God.*

The howling was downright scary—from the winds and the dogs now, both of whom were reacting.

"I wish we could do something," she said. "I hate that it has to run its course. Who knows what's going on out there? The damage it's causing." Her eyes were wet from unshed tears.

He reached for her and she melted against him. "We just have to ride it out. I'm gonna go check on the animals."

"Keep your distance, just in case they spook," she said.

"Birdie and Bunny warned me about that," he said with something of a smile. He got out of the sleeping bag, immediately cold and missing being so close to Claire. His flashlight guiding the way, he walked to the far end of the barn and turned into the corral area, immediately spotting the big pink pig with his head half-hidden under some hay. "Good idea, buddy," he said.

In the next pen were the four goats, and they were all huddled against one another in the tiny house a volunteer had made for them and given to the Whitaker sisters for Christmas last year.

The llamas, Drama and Llama Bean, were standing and looking like nothing got them down. They both eyed him and stepped to the edge of the pen.

"It's almost over," he assured them. "Just got to get through tonight, and tomorrow everything will be better."

A good metaphor for life and tough times, he thought. He sent up a silent prayer that Birdie and Bunny and the volunteers and all the Furever Paws animals were holding up okay, then he came back into the main area of the barn.

With the tornado roiling toward them, they'd just have to huddle together like the goats and hope like hell the damage was minimal.

Matt lay back down in the sleeping bag, and Claire did the same, this time facing the dogs. He spooned against her, his arm around her, and she grabbed on to his hand. Their flashlights were within reaching distance, next to their backpacks and water bottles, in case they needed to make a quick escape. He'd read that a tornado could last anywhere from a few seconds to an hour. He'd also heard on one news station that a recent tornado had lasted for *three* hours.

"It sounds like a freight train," she said, her voice choked.

He pulled himself tighter against her, holding on for dear life. He'd made a promise to himself and Claire— without her knowing it—that he wouldn't touch her, that he'd keep his hands and lips to himself. He wanted to break that promise right now, but he knew come morning, when everything was a wreck, he'd need to be strong for her, the sisters and for the animals.

Besides, he'd have to walk away soon enough. So keep his hands to himself, he would.

Claire's eyes popped open in the dark. Matt was silent and unmoving beside her; he'd stayed up well past

2:00 a.m., a fact she knew because that was the last time she'd jerked awake from the noise and he'd wrapped his arm around her, burrowing his chin into her hair. Every time he'd done that, she'd felt safe and secure enough to actually fall asleep, but she had a feeling Matt hadn't slept a wink.

Before she'd driven out to the barn, she'd put on her old battery-operated watch just in case the power went out, and she was glad she did. It was almost four o'clock now. The winds were howling. She'd heard crashes earlier, possibly trees falling, and she prayed the big oaks on the property wouldn't land on any of the buildings. The tornado had stopped, and she was glad Matt had finally fallen asleep. It was pitch-dark outside, the rain still beating down and the thunder still crackling.

His eyes opened, and he seemed to be straining to listen. "The howling stopped. Still pouring, though."

"We made it through."

He grabbed the smaller flashlight and shone it on the dog bed. Hank and Blaze were curled up tightly next to each other. "They seem okay."

She nodded. "I'm so glad they had each other for the worst of it."

"Like us," he said.

"Like us," she agreed.

She could barely see him in the dark, but she could feel him, breathing beside her, the very presence of him. They were just inches apart.

"I want to go out there with the flashlight and assess the damage," he said.

"In the morning," she whispered. "The flashlight

can't illuminate everything, and who knows what debris is out there or broken branches that could fall any minute."

He nodded. "I had a nightmare earlier. Not the same one I used to have about the explosion. This time it was about you."

"Me? I'm the subject of your nightmares? Great." She tried to inject some levity into her voice, afraid he'd turn away from her and go curl up with the dogs.

"You were running in the dark, thunder booming around you and lightning streaking above your head. Tree limbs were falling everywhere. I was standing up ahead and you were running toward me, but you never got closer. It was so strange. I couldn't move a step toward you. I was scared to death you were going to be hurt right in front of me."

"Was I?"

"I woke up," he said.

"What do you think the dream meant?" she asked. Because if he was about to read too much into it, she wanted to be able to refute his interpretation.

"It means what it is."

"What it is?" she repeated. "What is it?"

"That I'm supposed to let you go, even if I don't want to."

Now she was glad she asked. "You're not *supposed* to. You're *choosing* to, Matt. *You're* the one standing in our way. Your way."

"For good reason," he said.

"No, for no reason."

"I really love you, Claire," he said, his voice breaking. "I always have. But you've always deserved better."

"I don't get a say?"

He shook his head. "You're romanticizing the past. You always were a romantic."

"Me? Hardly. You're the romantic, Matt. Except in this case, you're turning our would-be love story into an almost-tragedy."

"I'll stay in town long enough to help Birdie and Bunny with any cleanup efforts, but then I'm leaving."

"Great. Hurt us both. Good going, Fielding."

"When you're married to a great guy who can give you the world, you'll be glad I was willing to walk away."

"I don't want the world, Matt. I just want you. I've only ever just wanted *you*."

He shook his head again, but she reached both hands to his face and kissed him so that he couldn't say anything else. No more talking. No more. He was leaving. Their second chance was a lost cause. She would have to accept it.

"Do something for me, then, Matt," she whispered.

"Anything."

"Give me a last night with you. Let's just have tonight and then you can go."

"I made myself promise I wouldn't touch you."

"You get to change your own rules," she pointed out. *Please let that sink into his stubborn head. You get to change your own rules.*

"You have no idea how much I want you," he said.

"Show me, then," she said.

He kissed her, peeling off her thermal shirt. His warm hands on her skin were electrifying. She reached down and undid the tie on the waistband of his sweatpants. And then he moved over her, his hands and mouth everywhere.

"Are you sure?" he whispered in her ear, trailing kisses along her collarbone.

"I'm sure," she said.

And then, after retrieving a little foil packet from his wallet, he made her forget all about the storm, all about his stubbornness, all about the fact that he'd be leaving in a matter of days, once again with her heart.

Chapter Fourteen

Matt opened his eyes, aware of only the silence and Claire's gentle breathing as she slept beside him.

Silence.

He gently touched Claire's shoulder. "Hey, sleeping beauty."

She opened her eyes, then bolted upright. "It's quiet."

"Exactly."

Well, it was quiet if you didn't count the pig oinking in his pen at the far end of the barn. Someone wanted breakfast.

"Let's go see what's going on outside, and then we'll check on the barn animals," she said.

They both shimmied out of the sleeping bag and rushed to the barn door.

"Wait," he said, Claire's hand ready to open the door. "We need to prepare ourselves. It could be really bad."

"I know."

The dogs padded over, Blaze looking much perkier than he had last night.

"Careful, guys," Matt said. "We'll go out first and make sure it's safe for your paws. Stay."

The dogs listened as Claire opened the door and sunlight poured into the barn. She looked out. "Oh no. Oh God. Matt."

She stood there, shaking her head, looking all around.

Devastation was the only word for the scene outside. Trees were torn from their roots and lying sideways across the property. One had even fallen on the roof, but luckily, it hadn't damaged the barn as far as he could see. The tornado had touched right down on Whitaker land, and had taken many of the huge old oak trees.

"Over here, Hank and Blaze," he said, allowing the dogs out in a safe area to do their business. The dogs seemed careful about stepping over branches and debris.

"Oh God, Matt, the shelter. What if—"

They could see the back of the building from where they stood, but not the front or the sides. They ran over, navigating through the downed tree limbs.

Birdie and Bunny stood in front of Furever Paws, their arms around each other's shoulders.

"Birdie! Bunny!" Claire called.

The Whitaker sisters turned around. Tough Birdie looked like she might cry. Bunny did have tears in her eyes as she shook her head.

"Somehow our farmhouse was barely affected," Bunny said. "We got darn lucky."

"The shelter fared worse," Birdie said. "Right in the path of those huge oaks. There's serious damage to the roof," she added, pointing at where a big section had been blown off and now rested against some trees in the forested area. "And a lot of fencing is gone."

"A few of the storage sheds were blown away—one slammed into a tree and seems to have half pulled it up from the ground."

"But you and the volunteers are okay?" Matt asked. "All the animals are okay?"

"All of us are fine," Birdie assured him.

"Same with the barn animals," Claire said. "And these two," she added, gesturing to where Hank and his shadow, Blaze, sniffed around.

"Well, we sure could use your help walking all the dogs," Birdie said. "Why don't we start with the ones in the farmhouse, and then we'll go see if the volunteers in the shelter basement are awake yet."

The four of them went into the farmhouse, Matt grateful the beautiful white home hadn't been hit. In the basement, they each headed for a kennel, Matt going for the little chiweenie, Tucker. As they stepped back outside, letting the dogs stretch and walk around a bit, he was amazed that so much sunshine could follow such turbulent weather. It was early, barely seven, and chilly, but the day promised to be warmer than it had been lately.

"The fenced play area is sound," Bunny said. "So

why don't we put these guys in there and go see how the dogs in the shelter basement fared."

"You two also," Claire said to Hank and Blaze, closing the gate behind them.

Once the dogs were secured, and Matt made sure that none of the trees were possibly near enough to come crashing down on the shelter or play area, they all headed inside the shelter. The section of the roof that had been damaged was in the lobby, toward the side where the gift shop had been. Thankfully, Birdie and Bunny had packed everything and secured it, so nothing was damaged, except the table where people would sit to fill out applications; it lay on its side, and there was some bad water damage from where the rain had come in. *It could be a lot worse*, Matt thought.

Just as they were about to head into the basement, the door leading downstairs opened, and two women stood there. "Boy, are we glad to see you all," one said. Matt hadn't met these women before yesterday, but he couldn't be more grateful to them for staying with the animals. There were five dogs down there, and they all trooped down the stairs to bring them up on leashes.

Finally, with those dogs settled in the play yard with the others, Birdie and Bunny hugged the two volunteers, who were anxious to leave and check on their homes.

With the volunteers gone, Matt, Claire and the Whitaker sisters stood in the fenced yard, watching the dogs play. Even Tucker, who usually kept to himself, seemed glad to join the reunion, sniffing at a gentle shepherd mix's ankles.

"Just based on the roof and the fencing alone, I'm

thinking we're looking at around twenty thousand in damages," Birdie said, eyeing the roof of the shelter.

Bunny shook her head. "Thank goodness for solid insurance. *And* that no one was hurt. Boy, did we get lucky."

Birdie nodded. "And we haven't walked the entire property—more downed trees might need hauling away."

"I hate this," Matt said. "Furever Paws and Whitaker Acres are so special and necessary, they should be untouchable. Even from acts of God."

Birdie put a hand on his arm. "This is how it goes, though, isn't it? Things get damaged and rebuilt, and life goes on."

He felt like she was talking about him. He *knew* she was. But some things were too damaged. Like himself.

Claire stared at him, as if hoping the wise Birdie had gotten through to him, just like she'd been trying to do for weeks now. Why did he feel so stuck? Part of him wanted to grab Claire and tell her he loved her, that he wanted to be with her, build a life with her. But part of him just couldn't. So he stayed silent.

"Let's go take a walk farther up," Bunny said. "See how bad it is up near the road."

So much debris, Matt thought as they surveyed the land. He saw lids from garbage cans that weren't Whitaker property, window shutters from God knew where. And so many tree limbs.

"Oh Jesus, is that a dog?" Matt said, his heart stopping.

"What? Where?" Claire said, looking at him, her beautiful green eyes frantic.

"Under that big tree branch," he said, pointing up ahead. A skinny black dog lay unmoving under the heavy branch. His eyes were open and he closed them every now and then, the only indication he was alive.

"Oh God, it is," Bunny said. "He's trapped. Poor thing looks like he gave up the struggle to free himself. Not that he could, given the weight of that tree limb."

"He's probably injured," Birdie said. "But how are we going to get the limb off him without bringing down the entire tree on him?"

Matt stared up at the rest of the tree, hanging in such a precarious position that could it could come toppling down any minute.

"I've never seen this dog before," Birdie said. "I sure as hell hope someone didn't abandon it before the storm." She shook her head, anger flashing in her blue eyes.

"Maybe the thunder or the tornado spooked him, and he ran off from his home and then got hit and trapped by the limb," Claire said. "I can't tell if he has a collar."

Matt couldn't see either. "I have to help him. Somehow, someway."

"I don't know Matt," Birdie said. "We might have to call in our tree guy with his heavy equipment."

Matt shook his head. "If he can even *get* here. We don't know how bad the roads are. And even if he could get here, the dog can't have much longer."

I'm going to help you, he said silently to the dog as he advanced slowly toward the downed tree, his heart beating a mile a minute.

"If you touch anything, that hanging branch could

come crashing down on both your heads," Bunny warned.

He stared at the injured, scared dog and saw himself. Claire, Sparkle, Hank, his sister and Ellie, the Whitaker sisters, Zeke and Bobby—they'd all reached out to him and brought him back to himself. Now he was going to help that dog.

Fear can't stop me, he thought. *Not from saving that dog. Not from life.*

Or from love. Because as Claire said, love is all there is. It makes everything else work.

He sucked in a breath and turned back to look at Claire, to drink in the sight of her for sustenance. She believed in him—she'd always believed in him. And she'd helped him believe in himself. He was getting that tree limb off that dog. End of story.

"I have some experience from my time overseas," Matt assured everyone, moving closer to the dog, his gaze going from the precarious tree limb to the dog's frantic eyes. "We were hit with all kinds of hard stuff in our path."

"Oh God, be careful," Claire said.

"I will," he said. He looked at the dog. "I'm coming for you," he said. "I'm going to get you out."

One wrong move and that tree limb would take them *both* out—permanently. *You can do it*, he told himself. Slow and steady. Then quicksilver. In a flash he thought about coming home to Spring Forest, the shock of seeing Claire. How a little girl's birthday wish of a puppy had completely changed his life. *What if I'd told my sister I didn't know anything about dogs and left it to*

her to choose a pup? I likely never would have run into
Claire. I certainly wouldn't have trained Sparkle. Or
adopted Hank. Or volunteered at Furever Paws and
met the Whitaker sisters.

I wouldn't be here right now.

Save that dog, he told himself.

"Matt," Claire said—from right behind him. "I'm
going to help you."

He was about to say *no, you could get hurt*, but he
could see the insistence in her eyes. She was determined. And Claire Asher didn't care about getting
hurt—she was front-line material.

Yes. She was.

He held out his hand and she took it.

They walked over as silently as they could, since it
was clear that any movement would topple the limb. He
kept his eyes warm and on the pooch, who was staring
at him, half-frantic, half-resigned to his fate—which
probably hadn't been all that great till this point.

He calculated where to best lift the limb pinning
the dog and noted a branch hanging precariously, just
barely attached to it. "I'll lift and you drag the dog
out," he said.

She nodded. "Got it."

"You might get bitten," he warned.

She waved a hand. "Hazard of life."

He stared at her and reached out a hand to her cheek,
then turned his attention back to the heavy limb trap-
ping the dog.

"We've got this," she said, holding his gaze.

He believed her.

"On my count, pup, okay?" he whispered to the dog. "One. Two. Three."

Before three had finished echoing in his head, he used every bit of strength he had—and a hell of lot in reserve—and lifted the limb up. Claire grabbed the dog under his front arms and pulled him clear.

His arms about to burst, Matt dropped the limb, and the hanging branch came crashing down right on the spot where the poor stray had been.

His heart was booming. He stood, his eyes closed, his legs buckling, his bad leg unable to deal.

"Oh, Matt," Claire said, rushing over, cradling the dog against her chest. "You did it. We did it. This sweet dog did it." She kissed the top of the dog's head, stroking its clumped, wet fur.

"I'll take him," Birdie said, stretching out her arms. "*Her*, actually," she added, as Claire transferred the dog to her arms. Bunny must have run to the barn for a towel, because she wrapped the poor thing up as Birdie shifted her in her arms. The dog looked so relieved to be warm and drying off.

"I'll call Doc J and see if he can come right away," Birdie said. "Her leg looks injured."

She and Bunny rushed the dog back into the shelter.

"You can take the man out of the army, but you can't take the army out of the man," Claire said.

He grabbed her to him and held her, relishing the feeling of her arms tightening around him. "We're all okay," he said, hearing the wonder in his own voice.

"We're all okay," she repeated, placing her hands on either side of his jaw.

His mind had gone as jelly-like as his legs, so he

let himself sit back and catch his breath, let his heart rate come back down to normal. But nothing was normal anymore. Not Furever Paws or the Whitaker land stretched out before him, devastation as far as the eye could see.

And not him.

Claire kept glancing at Matt as they all waited for Doc J to arrive to check on the injured dog. Matt had been very quiet since they'd gone inside to join the others. Now it was just the two of them in the shelter's examination room—and the dog, of course, a female mixed-breed that lay on a padded exam table.

Birdie had said it was a good sign that the dog had accepted a few treats from her, and her eyes did look brighter now that she was safe, though it was clear she was in pain. Right now, the dog seemed content to lay there without being pinned by the heavy tree limb, her rescuers cooing at her, petting her side.

Claire didn't know how she didn't melt into a puddle on the floor, her heart was so overflowing with love for this man.

Birdie and Bunny had gone out to the yard to check on the dogs, and make a plan for what to do with everyone until the roof could be taken care of and all the fencing restored.

"You're going to be okay," Matt said to the dog, gently patting its side. "You're in the best possible place now. Doc J will get you fixed up, and then someone will give you a good home. You'll be fine."

The dog gave Matt's hand a lick as he reached to scratch her ears.

Matt smiled. "No thanks necessary. Anyone would have done it."

"But you did," Claire said. "And whether you like it or not, Matt Fielding, you're going to have to listen to me tell you that you're more of a man than any I've ever known. And I love you. I know you're not a coward, so if you do leave Spring Forest and leave me, it's not because you're scared of commitment or love. It's because you don't love me. I get that now."

His mouth dropped open. He'd been a coward when it came to her. Afraid to let himself *feel* what he truly felt. Afraid to let himself have something so precious.

"I do love you," Matt said, looking into her eyes. "I absolutely do love you, Claire Asher."

"But…" she prompted, waiting for it. Bracing herself, tears poking her eyes and her heart so heavy she was about to drop to the floor.

"Not *buts*," he said. "I just love you. And you're right, I'm not a coward. So why the hell would I leave Spring Forest when everything I love is here? When you're here." He walked over to her and held out his arms. She rushed into them, closing her eyes, reveling in the feel of his arms around her, holding her tight.

"I truly thought I had nothing to offer you, and you showed me that I do," he said. "I'm just sorry it took me so long—and a tornado—to see it."

Claire smiled. "I call that the silver lining."

He reached both hands to the sides of her face and stared at her with so much love, so much intensity in his eyes, it was almost too much to bear. She'd seen that look before, when they'd been very young and deeply in love, no cares in the world. Now there were cares, but the look remained. She called that serious progress. "Eighteen years later, will you do me the honor of becoming my wife and sharing your life with me?"

Okay, now she was crying. "Yes. Yes, yes, yes."

"And, Claire, remember when I said a long, long time ago that if we had a baby I'd want to name him Jesse, after my brother?"

She held her breath. "Yes, of course I remember." She remembered what else he'd said too. *Not* that long ago.

"Let's have a baby," he said. "It's lucky that Jesse would work for a boy or a girl."

"Baby Jesse," she repeated, wrapping her arms around him. She put her head on his chest and stayed like that for a good minute. "Oh, Matt? I do have one request for our new life together."

"Anything," Matt said.

"If no one claims our new buddy here, I'd like to foster her—I'd like *us* to foster her—once she's given the okay by Doc J." Birdie had checked for a microchip and there wasn't one, but protocol meant alerting lost dogs websites and hanging flyers and waiting five days to see if anyone would come looking for her. Then she could be put up for adoption. But she'd need nursing back to health and training—and that was Claire Asher's specialty.

"Sounds like a great idea to me," he said. "I have a good name for her too, if the Whitaker sisters will give up naming rights. Hope."

She grinned. "Hope is a great name. A perfect name for her."

Just then, the black dog on the table let out a little

bark as if she agreed. Claire's eyes widened. "She likes the name!"

"Sparkle, Hank and Hope can be our ring bearers," he said. "And Blaze, unless he finds his forever home before then."

"Absolutely," Claire said, laughing. "And all our favorite dogs can be invited. Think they'll sit during the ceremony?"

He laughed. "I don't know about that, but I do know something." He put his arms around her shoulders.

She tilted her head. "Oh yeah? What?"

"That *I* found my forever home," Matt said, just as Hope let out another bark of agreement.

* * * * *

*Look for the next book in the
Furever Yours continuity,*
How to Rescue a Family *by Teri Wilson.
On sale February 2019,
wherever Harlequin Special Edition books
and ebooks are sold.*

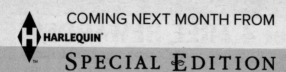

Get 4 FREE REWARDS!

We'll send you 2 FREE Books plus 2 FREE Mystery Gifts.

Harlequin® Special Edition books feature heroines finding the balance between their work life and personal life on the way to finding true love.

FREE Value Over **$20**

YES! Please send me 2 FREE Harlequin® Special Edition novels and my 2 FREE gifts (gifts are worth about $10 retail). After receiving them, if I don't wish to receive any more books, I can return the shipping statement marked "cancel." If I don't cancel, I will receive 6 brand-new novels every month and be billed just $4.99 per book in the U.S. or $5.74 per book in Canada. That's a savings of at least 12% off the cover price! It's quite a bargain! Shipping and handling is just 50¢ per book in the U.S. and 75¢ per book in Canada.* I understand that accepting the 2 free books and gifts places me under no obligation to buy anything. I can always return a shipment and cancel at any time. The free books and gifts are mine to keep no matter what I decide.

235/335 HDN GMY2

Name (please print)

Address   Apt. #

City   State/Province   Zip/Postal Code

Mail to the **Reader Service:**
IN U.S.A.: P.O. Box 1341, Buffalo, NY 14240-8531
IN CANADA: P.O. Box 603, Fort Erie, Ontario L2A 5X3

Want to try 2 free books from another series! Call 1-800-873-8635 or visit www.ReaderService.com.

---

*Terms and prices subject to change without notice. Prices do not include sales taxes, which will be charged (if applicable) based on your state or country of residence. Canadian residents will be charged applicable taxes. Offer not valid in Quebec. This offer is limited to one order per household. Books received may not be as shown. Not valid for current subscribers to Harlequin® Special Edition books. All orders subject to approval. Credit or debit balances in a customer's account(s) may be offset by any other outstanding balance owed by or to the customer. Please allow 4 to 6 weeks for delivery. Offer available while quantities last.

Your Privacy—The Reader Service is committed to protecting your privacy. Our Privacy Policy is available online at www.ReaderService.com or upon request from the Reader Service. We make a portion of our mailing list available to reputable third parties that offer products we believe may interest you. If you prefer that we not exchange your name with third parties, or if you wish to clarify or modify your communication preferences, please visit us at www.ReaderService.com/consumerschoice or write to us at Reader Service Preference Service, P.O. Box 9062, Buffalo, NY 14240-9062. Include your complete name and address.

HSE19R

#1 *New York Times* bestselling author

LINDA LAEL MILLER

presents:

**The next great contemporary read from
Harlequin Special Edition author Brenda Harlen!
A touching story about the magic of creating a
family and developing romantic relationships.**

*The cutest threesome in
Haven is still in diapers.*

Opening Haven's first boutique
hotel is Liam Gilmore's
longtime dream come true,
especially when he hires
alluring Macy Clayton as
manager. Good thing the
single mother's already
spoken for—by her adorable
eight-month-old triplets!
Because Liam isn't looking
for forever after. Then
why is the playboy rancher
fantasizing about a future with Macy and her trio of tiny
charmers?

**Available January 15,
wherever books are sold.**

HSE57358

"You kissed me," he reminded her.

"The first time," she acknowledged.

"You kissed me back the second time."

"Has any woman ever not kissed you back?" she wondered.

"I'm not interested in any other woman right now," he told her. "I'm only interested in you."

The intensity of his gaze made her belly flutter. "I've got three kids," she reminded him.

"That's not what's been holding me back."

"What's holding you back?"

"I'm trying to respect our working relationship."

"Yeah, that complicates things," she agreed. Then she finished the wine in her glass and pushed away from the table. "Will you excuse me for a minute? I just want to give my mom a call to check on the kids."

"Of course," he agreed. "But I can't promise the rest of that tart will be there when you get back."

She gave one last, lingering glance at the pastry before she said, "You can finish the tart."

He was tempted by the dessert, but he managed to resist. He didn't know how much longer he could hold out against his attraction to Macy—or if she wanted him to.

Had he crossed a line by flirting with her? She hadn't reacted in a way that suggested she was upset or offended, but she hadn't exactly flirted back, either.

"Is everything okay?" he asked when she returned to the table several minutes later.

She nodded. "I got caught in the middle of an argument."

"With your mom?"

"With myself."

His brows lifted. "Did you win?"

"I hope so," she said.

Then she set an antique key on the table and slid it toward him.

Don't miss
Claiming the Cowboy's Heart *by Brenda Harlen,*
available February 2019 wherever
Harlequin® Special Edition books and ebooks are sold.

www.Harlequin.com